Death for a Starter

Winner of the Best

Historical Thriller Award 2014

Reprint 2018

With love to my wife and best friend Jean. My grateful thanks for all the hours spent re reading and editing.

Also my appreciation to:

Derek Cook for the cover design

Death for a Starter

Death for a Starter

ISBN-13 978 1 9164697 2 3

Percychatteybooks Publishing

© Percy W Chattey 2014

**Percy W Chattey has inserted his right under the
Copyright, Designs and Patents Act, 1988,
to be identified as the author of this work.**

All rights reserved

This book is sold subject to the condition that it shall not by
way of trade or otherwise, be lent, resold, hired out, or
otherwise circulated without the publishers prior consent in
any form of binding or cover other than that in which it is
published and without a similar condition including this
condition being imposed on the subsequent purchaser.

All characters and events in this publication are fictitious and
any resemblance to any person living or dead is purely
coincidental

Death for a Starter

By the same Author

My friend Henry

Living in Spain

Politically Incorrect

(Voted best Thriller in the Pinnacle Awards)

Blitz & Pieces

(Voted best Autobiography in the Pinnacle awards)

The Black Venus

(Voted best Fiction in the Pinnacle Awards)

Watchit!

Watchit Too!

Time Gemtelmen

Death for a Starter

(Voted best Historical Fiction in the Pinnacle)

The Dauntless Factor

The Cormack's

Chapter One

The Mid Eighteen Hundreds

The Starter

Ireland - The O'Dowd's Small Holding

Alicia was desperate as she searched for food for her two children, Patrick and Florence. The ground was wet and very muddy. Her feet were icy, in shoes which were badly worn, giving little protection against the bitter cold. She was digging with her bare hands and holding a medium size sharp pointed knife to help in moving the soil to one side, trying to find a potato that had survived the blight. With a heavy heart she could see the fungus had spread across the plot of land, and that the leaves had wilted turning to a dirty looking brown

Death for a Starter

with round blackish spots. Although knowing it was useless, with her husband and son, both of whom were on other areas of the patch of ground, continuing their search for just one of the vegetables which had survived the disease.

She was feeling very tired, as it was almost a week since Alicia had eaten a fulfilling meal and the lack of proper food was starting to tell on her health. She looked up and her heart missed a beat as Reuben was holding up something, and in that moment Alicia knew he had found one that had survived the infection.

It had started to rain in a soft drizzle, like a heavy mist, as he started to make his way towards her. Tears flooded her eyes as she looked at the man she loved, and saw what the years, this terrible food shortage and constant worry had done to him. When they had married ten years previously they had so much hope. She had expected to continue the life she had had with her parents, living in luxury without having to work. In those days he was a strong man who stood tall – right now as he staggered across the field he was stooped, dressed in rags with mud over his legs and arms, looking far older than his years.

The hope vanished from her when she saw what he had in his hand. Although a full size potato she knew in her heart as soon as they cut into it the flesh would be inedible. Large tears ran down her cheeks as she flung her arms around him and cried on his shoulder. The rain adding to their depression as the cold water fell on each head and ran down the back of their necks.

Death for a Starter

"Mather" - it was their son Patrick. He like them had been working on another part of the small holding and he was calling beside the little cottage they called home. The stone built structure with its thatched roof was not very secure against the weather, a small building like so many others that had been built across the Irish countryside. Inside were just two tiny rooms where they lived, straw mattresses on the floor at night and during the day rickety wooden furniture littered the rooms for comfort of the barest minimum. In one corner was a small fireplace, which was rarely lit, as they could not afford to buy the fuel for it, and what kindling they could find in the fields surrounding them, was too wet to light for the warmth of a fire.

From the far side of their home she could see a well-dressed man on a black horse which was travelling down the narrow path. She knew at once it was the Land Agent, the man responsible for collecting rent and to do the bidding of the English Landlord. But this was a person she did not recognise. She turned and looked at her husband, "Who is he? What do you think he wants?"

"It has to be somebody about the rent and no doubt to check on the growth of their hay." Because they could not afford to pay rent the Landlord had allowed them to supply him with produce, which they had to grow from their own resources.

"But the growth has been so poor because of the foul weather - also I can't help feeling that the potato blight has

Death for a Starter

something to do with it. What can we do?" Alicia was frightened and knew this was not going to be good news.

A rare smile crossed his lips, "We have got nothing more to offer them." He took hold of her hand as they turned to struggle in the mud to the cottage.

The agent was a burly man who was smartly dressed in shiny boots and a leather jacket. He was holding a sword at his side as he dismounted from the horse, a completely black mare.

Once on the ground, he looked at them in distaste and turning, he took a board out of the pannier strapped to the horse behind the saddle. He looked at the paper attached to the board. "You have some land where your kind landlord has allowed you to grow hay instead of paying him rent. I need to see it, where is it?"

Reuben was shaking his head, "The seeds need some warmth for it to grow, it will look better when the weather changes." He had started to walk to one side of the cottage.

The agent was not pleased with what he saw, "Is this all?"

"Yes. When our farm was taken from us and we were told to farm this…(he waved his hands at the plot)…but the ground is too poor to grow crops on…" He wanted to shout at the man but knew it would be useless and would not help, instead his voice sounded weary and without conviction.

Death for a Starter

The agent turned and slapped him across the face. "How dare you, you ungrateful people. That grass had better recover very soon and be ready for the scythe." He then walked quickly to another part of their ground.

Alicia could feel the temper building inside her as she followed, the knife still in her right hand tucked out of sight up the rags of a sleeve.

"As you are not producing enough to pay the rent, this area will need to be turned into hay." He was pointing to a small plot on which a small skinny cow was grazing, the animal supplied the family with enough milk for them so they could survive.

"But that is not possible. Where would the animal go? There is no other place." Alicia was nodding her head as she listened to her husband.

"That is not our problem. You entered into an agreement, now stick to it." He turned to walk back to the horse, tucking the board under his arm, pushing Reuben out of the way as he did so. Reuben muttered "Forced into an agreement more like!"

Alicia moved and stood in front of him, "I suppose it does not matter to you if we die of starvation, as my Mother and Father did last year. All you want is our food and to leave us with nothing." She was talking slowly with tears running down her cheeks. She could not remember being so angry and furious at what this man was saying. She also knew, like so

Death for a Starter

many others they would not be able to continue to exist, which they were barely doing now. Without the feeble milk they were getting from the cow they would have nothing, and her children would suffer. It flashed through her mind - in that case why should he not suffer as well?

She stood her ground as he moved forward. She could hear her husband telling her to move out of his way. She shouted at the agent, "How do I feed the bairns? Eh! Go on tell me."

He was looking down at her grinning, "That is nothing to do with me," before he could say anything more she swung her right hand upwards. The knife, which she had been holding in her fist, with the blade held along her wrist could not be seen under the pieces of cloth she was wearing. Suddenly she reversed it, the blade flashed as she forced it upwards. There was a hesitation as it tried to penetrate the leather of the jacket. Using more vigour, the knife continued, the sharp pointed end went easily into him and continued up under his ribs.

There was no noise, just blood gushing out over the blade and her hand. With a surprised look on his face the agent silently dropped to the ground. Reuben looked at her astounded wondering what had happened; she was still standing and looking down in shock. She watched as Patrick pulled the blade from the visitor's chest, blood covering his hand and more on the rags he was wearing.

Death for a Starter

The agent lying on the ground had not moved. The couple standing beside the body were looking at each other, both wondering how it had happened whilst knowing they were in deep trouble.

There was a scream - Florence, their daughter had come out of the shack and was standing near them shivering, and starting to cry. Her mother took her in her arms rocking her and whilst still looking at her husband, her mind was in a whirl, knowing if and when the authorities found out they would all be hanged for murder.

Alicia in her heart knew what she had done was wicked, but what the man had intended was equally so, condemning a family to die from starvation like many others in that terrible time for Ireland. They both knew that now they had a death on their hands they would have to make a new start.

Chapter Two

The two parents were in shock. Reuben was looking around trying to find some inspiration for what to do next, all he could see was the low grey cloud and a bleak landscape with trees trying to recover from the wintry weather. He knew it was the last time he would set his eyes on the scene as they would need to move on, and very quickly. He could hear a voice and realised it was their son Patrick speaking. "Father, we have got to do something."

"What do you think son?" He looked down to the boy who was going through the pockets on the body removing papers and other items. Around the waist was a heavy leather belt, supporting the sword to one side, and on the other a black leather pouch with a large flap. Patrick lifted the flap and gasped.

11

Death for a Starter

The two adults looked down. In their son's hands was a large amount of money. They were stunned and yet relieved because both realised what Patrick was holding, if they could escape it could be their saviour.

The boy stood up and started to stuff the cash into a pocket he found in the rags he was wearing. "Father we have got to get this man out of sight, just in case someone comes along."

Reuben shook himself and tried to come to terms with what had happened. Turning to his wife and nodding to the body he said "Help me pull him into the cottage." They grabbed the agent by the shoulder and dragged the heavy weight into the stone building. With the task completed Reuben had a coughing fit, "We had better get the belt and other things that are recognisable off him. We can dispose of them later."

Alicia spoke, "What good will that do? He's dead he's not going anywhere."

"When it is dark, which will not be long now, we will leave him here. Gather what you want to take with you and we will burn the place, the roof will collapse in the heat and nobody will know who is inside the charred remains."

"What about the horse? And where would we go?"

"Turn him around and give him a smack on his back side and he will find his way home. My guess is that tomorrow

Death for a Starter

they will start to look for him." He coughed heavily as he pointed to the body.

"Hopefully when they come across the remains of this place he will be unrecognisable, and I cannot see people digging through the remains as everyone knows we have no valuables"

Patrick although not quite ten was tall and broad shouldered from the hard work he had had to do on the farm since he was a toddler. "Father, do you think we should go to the church – surely the Priest will help us?"

"I was thinking the same thing, son."

Patrick started to walk towards the agent's animal. "But first we should see what is in the panniers on the horse." Opening the flap he cried out, "There is more money in here."

The family were aghast with what they saw, Reuben said "Quick son get the old case that is the only way we are going to carry all this."

The church was more than an hour's walking distance. As soon as it was dark with the help of some dried hay, which they pulled from the roof, they set light to the little cottage that had been their home for so many hard and uncomfortable years. The family, each in their own way were sorry to leave. Florence went over to the small piece of grass and hugged the cow with tears in her eyes, for they knew if the situation was to be believable when someone came looking then they had to leave the animal. Before setting off they sent the horse on its

Death for a Starter

way, which with a snort went off at a fast trot seeming to know where it was heading.

It was very dark and cold, the young girl was moaning because she wanted to be carried - Dad obliged by lifting her on to his shoulders, having passed the case he was carrying to Alicia. Wrapped in some old sacking were the sword and other equipment the agent had been carrying on his person. Before getting to the little town of Tullamore they would cross the Offaly River over a narrow stone bridge. When they reached the crossing Patrick was given the bundle and told to walk along the river bank a little way before throwing the bundle into the water, which by past knowledge they knew to be very deep.

Patrick looked at the sword and had a strong desire to keep it but knew it would be easily recognised. Looking at it with longing, he took a deep breath and hurled it into the water.

**

The O'Dowd's nearest neighbour lived over a mile away across the flat landscape in a small house. The wife was sitting at a table carrying out some repairs to clothing - at the time sewing up a hem, when she saw the flames coming from the cottage across the fields. The couple looked at each other, the old farmer saying, "I knew they were having a hard time, but what now. If I go over there by the time I get there it will be too late - I do not see what I will be able to do. But someone may need help." He was pulling on his boots as he said it.

The wife went to the fire burning in the grate and stoked the embers and pushed the stew pot over to the griddle to warm it up. "If they need anything I'll be happy to help. There is still some stew left over they will be welcome to that. They can stay in the barn, at least it is dry."

The farmer left, trudging down the little used track between the two properties. By the time he got to the burning cottage nearly half an hour had past, the flames had died down and only a pile of glowing embers inside the walls was all that could be seen, these were left from the roof which had collapsed into the interior. He called their names a few times and getting no reply, he could not see the point in hanging around and turned to make his way back. On seeing the old white cow with coloured brown spots he released her tethers and led it away.

Returning to his wife he said, "There's no sign of them, unless they were inside the cottage if so they are goners. I brought their animal back with me, if they are still alive then they will want it."

**

Finally, very tired after the walk the family entered the church, it was no warmer inside than it was outside, and their voices echoed around the vaulted ceiling. They sat in a line in one of the pews near to the altar, kneeling down and

Death for a Starter

praying, each individual murmuring softly into their hands using their own words for comfort.

Footsteps approached them. Reuben looked up fearfully. A feeling of relief came over him as he saw the Priest looking down at them, with his hands clasped in front of him.

They all started to apologise but the man of the church held his hands up. "I can see you are in need of some help. How long is it since you have eaten?"

After their reply he said, "Then we must put that right, but first I think you would be happier if you were cleaned up."

It had been a long while since they had been so comfortable. The Priest was an elderly man with white thinning hair with which he had a habit of pushing it away from his eyes. He welcomed them into the sanctuary of his home, and immediately knew these people were different from others that sought help from the church, they looked tired but above all frightened.

His first task was to allow them to be cleaned up and remove the mud that was caked onto them. He asked if they could pay for clothing as there was a woman in the town who could supply them. Being assured that money was no problem, which surprised him, but also confirmed in some way what his first thoughts were. Whilst they were bathing in the cold water of his simple bathroom, he vanished for a short time and when

Death for a Starter

he returned he had an assortment of clothing to replace the rags they were wearing.

It was the following day when the holy man left them, explaining the need to visit some of the elderly in the town bringing them comfort and prayer. Before leaving he spoke to Reuben who again, had been coughing. "I'll see if I can get some mixture for that cough there is a person locally that produces medicines."

While he was gone they were fearful that he would bring the local constable back with him. Reuben was wondering what they would do if that happened. But that was not to be, when the priest returned he handed over a bottle with a liquid in it, before saying, "This should help with that cough." He was smiling when he continued. "There is a story amongst the folks that a family of farmers have died in a house fire. Another story being told, of an agent of the land an owner has disappeared, and of course he would have had a lot of money on him."

As if the story was not related to them he carried on. "In a few days a friend will take you to the canal. It is not too far but we must wait for the timing of the barge. From there you should be able to arrange passage on one of the vessels that regularly goes to Dublin itself. I feel sure you will be able to pay for your journey. But be careful the English have eyes everywhere. If I was in your position, with the risk you are running, that is where I would go - England. Nobody will be surprised as many people are going there because of this dreadful famine." He smiled once more at them, "I have some

Death for a Starter

work to do - oh and by the way the church is very poor and if you could help out a little it would be appreciated."

The O'Dowd's knew they had been very lucky and what the Priest had said made sense. They also knew they would have to trust him for it was obvious he knew who they were. So they decided that they should follow his advice and agree to what he had suggested. It was a few days later when a local man with a horse and buggy arrived, to take them to the canal for their passage to Dublin, the capital city.

Before leaving the vicarage they said their farewells to the Priest and gave him a donation for the church funds, for which he was very grateful. Then he said "Be careful the local constable is looking into the missing agent, the sooner you leave Tullamore the better." He paused "But first I think we should say a prayer for the departed, especially Land Agents." They went down on their knees and prayed. Afterwards the man from the church said "One last thing which you should know - Dublin Castle, is the stronghold of the British rule. You should avoid it, as it is from there that they have many informers. I am going to ask you to leave by another door which cannot be seen from the road. If you wait outside the rear gate you will be collected from there." He bent over and kissed Alicia's hand, before turning around to leave them adding "Be very careful."

The driver was dressed in a long brown coat with a black felt bowler type hat, with a pair of reins in one hand whilst the other held a long handled whip. He was a man who handled the horse and cart expertly. Three of the family sat in

18

Death for a Starter

the back of the twin wheeled vehicle which rocked alarmingly as they clambered into it. Reuben climbed on to the seat next to the driver, coughing as he did so. The horse was encouraged to move off. The pair on the driving seat had little to say to each other. After a while the owner of the wagon said, "I understand the Landlord wants the cottage, which was destroyed in a fire, to be put back in to use. That cart with men on it which went the other way just now - they are on their way to clean it out and I am told there is someone waiting to move in." He added, "I noticed the local constable was sitting in the back of the cart he must be interested to see what happened out there." Their father had another coughing fit.

Reuben swallowed hard and knew they must get out of Ireland as soon as possible. To their advantage in the period of the mid 1800's, there was no central police force, just local constables who were employed by each individual authority to look after events in their neighbourhood.

Before they alighted from the cart, the carter said, "Now we know the constable is poking his nose in and no doubt will be asking questions, just to help my memory not to remember too many things. I think the fare should be more than we agreed."

The O'Dowd's knew they had no choice and came to an agreement with him and paid up.

**

Death for a Starter

The men arrived at the O'Dowd's old cottage. They walked around inspecting it and came to the conclusion that the walls were still sound and if they cleared the burnt embers from inside and replaced the roof, their work would be done.

The constable, Sean, stood around looking bored, but knew there were bodies in the ruin as the sickly sweet smell of decomposition was in the air. He held a not so clean handkerchief to his nose, whilst the other three started to clear the rubble from inside. The work was a dirty job with the soot from the burnt timbers rising in clouds every time they moved some of the larger pieces, and especially when sweeping the floor.

From time to time the policeman would ask if they had found any bodies, and as they got further and further into the burnt out wreck he was starting to get suspicious.

They were nearing the furthest part of the building, when one of them saw the remains of a body, and called the officer to come and take a look. He was not happy entering this dirty hole - the smell was awful, but he knew that he had to. When he saw the body he was at first satisfied that perhaps the family had perished here. But then he saw it was wearing boots – the type of boots which would have been polished and shiny, and he knew he had found the Land Agent.

Chapter Three

The family were surprised and astonished at the sights they were seeing on their travels. They were people who had never gone very far beyond their homestead and they were constantly amazed at their new experiences.

The barge was pulled along by a horse, which ambled along the tow path beside the canal and was changed for a fresh animal at regular stages. Florence, Alicia & Reuben's daughter would frequently walk beside the working animal, sometimes stroking its nose, as it pulled the large vessel behind it.

Whilst out patrolling, the local constable at Robertstown was riding near the canal and watched the barge

Death for a Starter

as it was manoeuvred under a road bridge, and re-attached to the tow horse as it slid from beneath the structure. A young girl had been helping to lead the animal from one side to the other and was stroking it whilst the harness was fitted in place.

The constable sat astride his mount and after watching the scene for a few moments he moved on. As he did so he pulled on the chain which was attached to a pocket watch in his waistcoat. Looking at the time he thought by now he should be having his usual drink in the bar of the Grand Canal Hotel, where travellers rested for the night before moving on the next day.

He was in his usual place in the bar of the hotel looking out across the canal, when the barge came into sight and stopped for the night. The little girl he had seen earlier in the day walking beside the horse, was holding a woman's hand as they came into the hotel. Behind them was a tall man slightly bent who was coughing between talking to a young boy. After a chat with the barge owner, for no other reason than he liked to know what was going on, he learned they and the other passengers were on their way to Dublin to catch the boat for England.

Over a week was to pass before they arrived in Dublin. After all the time they had spent on the slow small barge, Alicia along with Reuben was pleased to step on to the dockside in Dublin. They quickly learned that they would have to wait nearly seven hours before catching the ferry boat to England. As they wandered through the streets looking at the different variety of shops, Alicia was tempted to enter and

Death for a Starter

finally she gave up the struggle, pushing the door open to a ladies dress shop, insisting Rueben do the same in the gentlemen's outfitters nearby.

An hour was to pass when she emerged in her new outfit. There was a new case in her hand with more clothes in. She walked out of the premises' hardly recognising her husband who had been to the barbers and was now clean shaven with his hair combed into the latest fashion. Alicia had made sure her daughter had also been kitted out; Reuben had done the same for Patrick.

After stopping to have something to eat at a small eatery, they made their way to the landing stage to catch the overnight ferry. Reuben looked a lot better now he had been shaved and was dressed in decent clothing, but she was still worried about him as his cough seemed to be getting worse.

Again the family were overwhelmed with what they heard and saw as they were directed to the docks for their passage to England. They joined the other souls pushing and elbowing their way in a disorganised crowd, all wanting to leave the famine of the Irish countryside, most dreaming of a different life style in England. The majority wanted work so they could support their families, and had heard of jobs being plentiful as the mainland was building railways and other large projects.

In the crowd was a mixture of people - mostly men dressed in working clothes all carrying a small bundle with their personal things. The O'Dowd's stood out from most of

Death for a Starter

the travellers as they were now better dressed than they had ever had the fortune to be.

The crowd continued to push forward slowly. Alicia could see that it was being funnelled through a single gate. There were people standing around watching the passengers as they were processed before getting on the ship which was moored a little way along the quay. The O'Dowd's were nervous, both felt like turning around and running away from what they thought was a trap. Reuben was having a coughing fit again and people were looking at them.

Alicia was carrying Florence who had started to fret as the family finally arrived at the gate beside a small hut. Men and women had been shuffled into a single file and were being counted through.

The family was very worried, but when they got to the front of the queue they felt the joy of relief, as they were let through. No names were being asked for, and all the gate keeper was interested in was taking the fare from each one, and making sure that there were no more people than the boat could hold.

The two parents both realised their mistake by buying the new clothes; everyone around them was dressed poorly, very much to their discomfort as they stood out from the crowd. Alicia was dressed in a green matching outfit with a long skirt and jewellery at her neck and wrist whilst Reuben was dressed as if he was going to a ball - not the third class

Death for a Starter

overnight crossing on a ferry. Both were carrying cases which were so obviously brand new.

Leaving the small hut, the family followed the other prospective immigrants and walked along the quay to the gang plank. This was a series of swaying planks linked together over which they walked with care down to the vessel, one hand holding the luggage and the other gripping a rope which doubled as a hand rail. The rope was at waist height and swayed in the opposite direction to the footway, and sagged between the linked support posts leading them on to the steamer.

The ferry was a large vessel with three tall masts and a large funnel to its centre with huge paddle wheels on each side near the midpoint of the accommodation. There were two levels of fare; the cheaper of the two was to be on deck for the crossing which was about two thirds of the price of being below deck out of the weather. Reuben stated in the middle of a coughing fit that "They had already spent too much money that day," He insisted that he would make himself comfortable outside in the air, which he went on to argue, "The fresh air will do me good and help to stop the irritation in my throat". He got his way and the rest of the family went below into the questionable comfort of the lower deck.

**

Meanwhile in Dublin Castle - the seat of the British rule over Ireland - a man, straight backed and tall wearing a long dark coat with tails, holding his top hat under his arm as

Death for a Starter

he strode across the hallway, leaving his carriage by the entrance from the street. He had an air of authority about him. His manner was one of the 'Do not trouble me I know where I am going and I am in a hurry', as he skipped up the broad stairs leading to the upper floors.

He strode into an office and addressed the man sitting behind an oak desk. "Sir, we have a problem over the missing persons from Tullamore. We have had a report from the constable there – he says it was not the family that perished in the cottage fire - it was the Land Agent. They have found his body in the burnt out cottage and it appears he had been stabbed. So it is the O'Dowd family we are looking for."

"Have we got a description? The agent took out a note book and read out the description of the family.

With this information the authorities set out to find out what happened to the O'Dowd's, and in what direction they went. A hasty meeting was called and a group of detectives were given orders to look for the family.

They also knew when passengers went across to England, names were not taken and there were no records kept. But it was a different matter with the emigrant ships that sailed to the United States and other countries. The telegraph machines started to chatter to all outlets to see if they could trace where the family had gone.

**

Death for a Starter

In Tullamore - Sean, the local constable, had also received instructions as to find where the O'Dowd's had gone. He had heard rumours that the local carter had been seen travelling with strangers on his vehicle, so he called to see him.

"A few days ago you had some unrecognised folks in your cart. Where did you take them?"

"Let me see… what day would that have been?"

"Three days…four days ago – why?... I don't know. You tell me?"

The carter stood his ground shaking his head.

"Alright let's put it another way. Have you picked up any strangers recently and if so where did you take them?"

He realised that he could not deny it completely as the constable already knew – but he had liked the family and had said he would not tell tales. "Yes now I remember - there were four of them and they asked me to take them to the canal. That's right it was some time ago."

"Where had they come from - and where did they go?"

"Up near the church – I just told you they wanted to go to the canal and that is where I took them."

"What do you mean 'up near the church?'"

Death for a Starter

"That is where they were – I do not know where they came from."

Neither of them wanted to involve the priest or the church, so after little more questioning the constable was satisfied and went on his way.

Chapter Four

The coal fired steam engine which propelled the ship, situated somewhere below decks, came to life with grey water vapour spouting into the air from the funnel. The whole vessel started to shake and vibrate, and somewhere below decks there was the noise of glasses rattling. The crew and the shore men were walking at a quick pace, along the deck and the quay releasing the ropes that had secured the ship to the dock. With its whistle sounding, drowning out all other noises, the crafts' big paddle wheels started to revolve slowly as it moved away from the dock.

The ship progressed gently across the harbour with the water turning white behind it from the paddle wheels. Seagulls swept and dived at the stern searching for food, following the craft as it headed for the open sea. When it passed the mouth

Death for a Starter

of the harbour, the waves, no longer restricted by the haven of the port, started to make the vessel lift and sway and then plunge into the troughs.

Reuben felt very cold from the icy wind that was blowing, he had another coughing fit as the chilly air from the easterly airstream got into his lungs. He was starting to wonder at the wisdom of staying on deck just to save a few pennies when they had so much money, most of which was safely tucked in a money belt, around his wife's waist.

Below deck Alicia was feeling a little strange in her new clothes. After spending so many years in rags, this feeling was more than emphasised by her fellow passengers who were not so well dressed and would frequently glance in her direction. Once again she started to regret the spending spree they had in Dublin before queuing for the ferry and was wondering how to change her looks but could not find an answer to that problem. She had made herself secure on one of the wooden seats, Reuben's case as well as her own was standing on the deck by her feet. She was fidgeting and trying to get comfortable as she adjusted to the movement of the ferry. Florence was not very happy and was moaning as she cuddled her mother.

Patrick was interested in the workings of the ship and was walking around looking into things, occasionally being pushed around by the crowd and the rolling of the craft - dreaming that one day he would captain one of these boats and sail around the world, not realising that it was ships, not steamers, which covered the long distance routes.

Death for a Starter

Alicia, had been brought up in a very wealthy family and her new clothing reminded her of that period. As a child her up-bringing had been very strict, with frequent visits to church with her parents where she was indoctrinated in their way - with three elder brothers she had learned as a young child to defend herself against their high spirits. Nevertheless sex was a taboo subject, even after she was married which was soon after her twelfth birthday. It was not until sometime after, when her husband, who was five years older than her, wanted a child did Alicia let him near her.

Up on deck the wind had risen, and the boat was more unstable as it thrashed its way through the seas. Patrick was enjoying himself on his wanderings and hung on to the hand rails as he made his way onto the deck to check on his Father, who was not enjoying the ride and whose coughing had got worse.

Patrick returned to the lower deck where his mother was sitting, having pushed his way through the throng of other passengers. As he entered the saloon he was astonished to see a couple in a corner. The man was on top of her in a steady movement and there was a rowdy group standing round them clapping. He stood rooted to the spot, staring. Going over to his mother he asked what they were doing. Alicia held her hands up in horror turning her head away. "Don't look at them and don't you dare do anything to a girl like what is happening over there. I cannot explain, but when we get to Liverpool, we will join a church and no doubt the Priest will explain it to you. But don't you ever dare to think about touching a woman."

The young lad was stunned at the forceful way his mother had reacted. He turned and pushed his way up the gangway and on to the deck - he wanted to go to his Father and ask him, but found him coughing very badly and he could see blood on his jacket.

The ferry suddenly pitched more than normal and Reuben fell on to his side and rolled onto the floor. His son was in a panic, bending over the man he loved and respected but he immediately knew he was dead. He didn't know what to do - he tried to get some of the other passengers to help, but they refused. They were frightened of the disease that had struck his Father down.

A man in a scruffy uniform pushed him with his foot and Patrick watched as his Father rolled over the side into the water. Patrick pulled at the man's sleeve and shouted "What did you do that for?"

"Because boy he was dead and he died of something we don't want spreading around the ship. Are you on your own now?" Thinking maybe he could get a few bob for him when they got to Liverpool, by one of the men who traded in children.

"No - my mother is downstairs with my sister."

Death for a Starter

Disappointed, the crewman said, "I'll come with you to tell your mother what happened - she will need you for comfort."

The boy with tears in his eyes returned to his mother, sobbing as he told her what had happened.

Alicia looked up at the crewman, "What right did you have to do that" she screamed, "He was my husband…how do you know he was dead? You have probably murdered him – all he had was a cough - Why oh why?"

"I'm sorry Madam but he was very dead, he has been coughing very badly since we sailed - your boy will confirm that – he was dead there was blood all down his shirt where he had been coughing – lots of blood – no he was dead alright we could not risk any disease he had spreading around the ship".

She turned away from him and crossed herself and cried quietly holding her young daughter closely to her. In some way it was a relief, she would not have to dig in the ground looking for potatoes again, she would be able to return to a more easy life and do what she wanted now she had enough money to do it.

**

Dublin Castle stood with the afternoon sun shining on its façade. From its gates two men left the old building and walked quickly away. It had been established that if the O'Dowd's had caught the barge for the city it would have arrived a little earlier on that day. The two men were on their

Death for a Starter

way to find out, as it was thought, they may still be around. To their disappointment when they arrived at its terminus it had already begun the return journey, a couple of hours previously, and there was no sign of the wanted family.

They looked at each other, neither wishing to follow the vessel, but they had their orders to follow the barge so they would be able to question the master of the craft. It was getting very dark with black rain clouds gathering as they rode down the tow path. At first it was just gentle drops of water, but as they progressed the downpour that followed was intense.

They continued on, not talking trying to keep warm and dry, wrapped up in their dark green waterproof capes, but the water was getting past their defences and was gently making their inner clothes wet. The unpaved trail turned to thick mud and the horses were unable to find a grip for their hooves and were slipping in the mire. The two men dismounted and lead the animals. Normally it was a two day journey on horseback, but with the weather as it was, it was not until the third day that they caught up with the vessel when it arrived at Robertstown for the nightly stop.

Ross the local constable, after discovering who they were, was very happy to describe in detail the family of the little girl who liked stroking the noses of horses. The two English agents were cold and tired after their ordeal. They listened intently to what the local officer had to say and knew they had all the information they were going to obtain and returned to Dublin Castle.

Death for a Starter

After a discussion with their superiors, it was decided it was an Irish problem. They and others would keep a look out for the O'Dowd family who could be anywhere by now. The agents had other pressing problems to solve, so they filed away their papers.

Chapter Five

Liverpool England

As far as Alicia was concerned it had been a very sad and rough crossing, although some of the regular travellers had thought the opposite remarking how smooth it had been. Gathering their things around them, the trio, with mother leading left the ferry, only to find the people on the dock side were more violent than the passengers on the crossing.

Stepping off the equally swaying footbridge from the boat as the one when they boarded, she saw two men standing to one side. Holding the two cases in her hands she ushered the two children in the opposite direction, trying hard not to look at them but failing. As they started to walk towards her, she started to panic. A group of children dressed in rags were

36

Death for a Starter

in her way. They were holding their hands out shouting and pleading for money. She looked over her shoulder and the two men had stopped and were talking to someone who had come off the overnight ferry, much to Alicia's relief.

There were touts everywhere trying to sell all sorts of items from barrows or trinkets out of cases. Others had pictures of their wares, including semi clad ladies which Patrick had found fascinating and found difficulty in dragging his eyes away.

Alicia found she was attracting attention. Her two children were a little way behind her, she soon had a crowd around her. The people on the streets were in the most poorly dressed and recognised a well attired person who was different to the other passengers who could possibly have money.

few had tried to grab a case from her hand. There were also the pickpockets looking for ways of relieving people of their valuables. Unexpectedly a ruffian grabbed hold of her, forcing her against a wall. His hand was twisting the sparkling necklace in his fingers, tightening it around her wind pipe. His face was very close to hers staring her in the eyes. "Come on lady bitch tell me where your money is – tell me quick before I really hurt you?" Over the attackers' shoulder she could see her son coming quickly to her aid.

Patrick, had taken charge of the knife that had killed the agent, before they had left Tulllamore. He was grieving for his father when he observed his mother being attacked, his temper rose, how dare someone try and rob his mother. He pushed through the crowd drawing the blade from the scabbard at his waist as he did so.

He slipped his hand around the neck of the attacker and pulled him backwards towards him whispering in his right ear "You had better let her go or you are going to be very much dead." As he spoke he was pushing the point of the blade into the others back knowing that he must be feeling the point of the weapon penetrating his skin.

The rogue released his hand from Alicia's throat and Patrick pulled the knife away, aware that he would have marked the other man's back. As he did so he grabbed a handful of the mugger's hair. Pulling his face down, Patrick brought his knee up hard into the man's face.

Spinning round he held the knife out in front of him moving it in circles and looking at the crowd. The people who had gathered around the fracas saw a slim young man - broad at the shoulders and a powerful look in his eyes - hence they moved back out of his way. Pointing to where the horse drawn buses were parked in a row he said, "We are moving over there, and I don't want anyone coming near us." The crowd kept their distance, some looking at the man lying on the ground with blood pouring from his nose.

Although a few drivers with carriages offered their services, Alicia was careful and wanted to stay with the crowd and insisted they boarded a horse drawn tram that would take them into the centre of the city. Patrick was not too certain; he would have preferred somewhere less crowded. He had put the

Death for a Starter

knife back into its holder, and followed his mother keeping his eyes looking at the people around him and making sure his sister was always close to him.

The vehicle rocked and rattled along, stopping to let passengers get on or others to get off. It finally came to a halt in Queen's Square - the busy heart of the city. Alighting from the tram, they walked around looking at the street traders, taking in the atmosphere wondering at the sights. Without realising it, as the trio were busy looking at all the new places of interest around them, they were standing outside a tall building with a doorman stationed on the pavement. The word 'Hotel' did not mean a great deal to them, but when they discovered it was somewhere they could stay, they entered through the large twin doors with frosted glass panels into a tiled area. There was a desk at one end with a young woman standing behind it.

"Can I help you?" she asked. "The manager will not be very long." She was dressed very smartly in a long maroon dress in what appeared to be the colours of the premises.

"Is this somewhere where we can stay?"

The receptionist smiled, looking over her shoulder to see where the manager was but he was out of sight. She asked them "Of course. What is your name?"

It was not until then, did Alicia realise it would be prudent to use another name other than O'Dowd. Her maiden name had been Cormack, so stuttering a little she used that.

Death for a Starter

The receptionist smiled recognising the hesitation as a lie, "Will your husband be joining you?"

"No. He died on the boat on our way over from Ireland."

"Oh I see. I don't think we have a room for you, we don't accept ladies on their own."

"But I'm not on my own I have my two children with me."

"Yes so I see." The young girl was feeling sorry for them, knowing if they were arrested the horror for them would be something that would haunt her. Before speaking she looked over her shoulder again. "Well......." She hesitated, knowing that she could get into trouble for what she was about to say. Lowering her voice she said "You see we have been asked to look out for a family named O'Dowd. But of course that is not you, your name is Cormack. You look very nice decent people and I'm sure you will find somewhere else."

Before leaving, Alicia stuttered her thanks. And then, as quickly as they could, they made for the door. She was in a panic at what the girl had said, thinking it would be wise to move as far away as they could from the city and the docks. Ushering her two children out through the doors where she looked each way, conscious of the doorman looking at them trying to make up her mind about which was the best way to turn. She realised that she had a serious problem if the girl was

Death for a Starter

to say something. The police would know that there were only three of them.

They had some difficulty walking down the narrow cobbled streets which all had open drains in a gully. Sometimes this was in the centre of the roadway, at other times it would be to the side. All were flowing with foul smelling liquid. After a little while they knew they were totally lost in what was a completely alien situation, being pushed around and trying to stop having their bags dragged from them also the children in rags holding out their hands for treats.

It was with relief when they saw a Priest talking to a crowd of children who were gathered around him. The three of them approached the group asking the Father if he knew of somewhere they could stay. He smiled at them and pointed to what looked like a very run down property on a corner. "If you tell the owner I sent you she will find space for you. In the morning perhaps you would visit me in the church – it is down here - turn left and make your way down to the main road you cannot miss it - perhaps I will be able to help you some more."

Taking hold of her daughter's hand with a case in the other, she crossed the cobbled surfaced road with Patrick following, carrying the rest of their belongings. She stepped over the foul smelling drains and entered the house the Holy Father had pointed to. Their first thoughts were that it was not very clean, the floor was dirty and there were mouse droppings in the corners. But this was of no concern to them

Death for a Starter

after the horrors of what they had been through in the last few days.

They were shown to an available room after they had mentioned that the Priest had told them to go there. The elderly woman who ran the hostel led them up a narrow staircase. The room was small with two dirty stained thin mattresses on the wooden floor. There were no sheets just two shabby blankets, one of which was split in the middle. Nevertheless, it was somewhere to sleep, but Alicia could not help noticing that the woman would frequently look at the cases. Once again she wished she had not bought such obvious expensive items.

Shutting the rickety door there was no way to fix it, but she had noticed a chair in the hall which Alicia retrieved to wedge against it. She put the two cases at their heads and exhausted they curled up in the middle to keep each other warm and slept for the first time in many nights, not being aware of the scratching noises somewhere in the walls, or the noise when somebody tried to enter the room without success by pushing the door.

The following day, the owner directed her to the Catholic Church where they knelt in the pews and Alicia prayed. After a little while, the Priest arrived who they had spoken to the previous day. "I hope you slept well? Perhaps we will be able to find you somewhere a little bit more comfortable."

Death for a Starter

Alicia asked to be able to confess her sins. After leaving the confessional, she encouraged her two children to do the same.

We will not know what Alicia told the Priest, but when Florence went into the small box and started to talk to the holy man, she told him everything about the man on the big black horse, and how he fell to the ground, and having to leave their cow and watching their home burning down.

After which the elderly Priest wanted to talk to Alicia, "I think my child, you need help. We had some men here a few days ago and they were looking for a family. Would you object if I made arrangements for you to stay here for a while with my blessing?"

"Thank you Father. That would be a great help, but where would we stay?" She was looking around her at the interior of the small church as she said it.

"You could stay with the Sister in the Nunnery which is behind this church; they will be very pleased to look after you for a few days whilst we find a way out of your problem?"

The Priest was as good as his word and they were introduced to the Sisters who lived in a tall red brick building to the rear of the church. The nunnery had closed shuttered windows, and to the entrance closed and bolted large oak double doors with black steel studs covering them. After they had passed through the open door they heard the bolts being pushed back into place and the three of them entered the dark

Death for a Starter

interior where they were shown a section of the holy house which was put aside for guests. The following day Alicia left the home and started her quest for somewhere the family could live and call home.

.   Patrick had another mission although he was interested in what would be their new home; he was fascinated by the shops and some of the coffee houses. On the odd occasion he would leave the nunnery and wander around on his own, waiting for his mother to return who he knew was trying to find them a home. On his outings he was pleased to be in the fresh air despite the smells, and away from the stifling quiet of the Holy House.

On one of the days he was out exploring, Patrick strolled along a crowded street following the crowd. He looked at shop windows, listening to hawkers and peddlers selling their wares - men with long coats and top hats and women in long skirts and sometimes a hint of a petticoat showing and with differing shapes of bonnets on their heads. Others were less well dressed.   There were also the porters pushing carts or carrying baggage, all this was still so new to Patrick's mind. He had turned a corner and found himself outside a coffee house. He decided he would see what went on inside.

The pictures of the scantily dressed ladies on the front of the property made him feel strange. He pushed the door open to find the place very busy with men, all of whom seemed to be talking at the same time, the air was full of smoke from foul smelling pipes and cigarettes.

Death for a Starter

"What do you want boy? If you want a woman they are that way." A tall scruffy looking man smoking a pipe with smoke curling upwards was staring down at him. He had a grin on his face as he pointed towards a staircase, which Patrick could see through an archway.

Feeling as if the world was looking at him, he made his way across the room to where he had been directed; with a small thrill in his stomach he could see the stairs. Holding on to the hand rail as if his life depended on it, he slowly made his way up the badly stained carpeted steps. As he neared the top, he could see four women sitting on chairs chatting to one another on a large landing. When they saw him they exchanged glances.

He had reached the top step when one of them dressed in a flowery skirt reaching just below the knee and a tight bodice said "Hello son – what can we do for you?" She paused still looking at him. "Have you got a problem with that thing you've got in those breaches?"

He started to stutter but in his embarrassment the words would not come. He decided to leave. Turning, he quickly went back the way he had come, tripping over a few steps in his flight. He heard laughter from behind. As he went through the bar he was sure everyone was staring at him.

Chapter Six

It was almost four months since they had arrived and after many weeks of difficult travelling around the area, Alicia was in a horse and trap. The Agent she had been introduced to was driving, and they were on their way to see a property near the small market town of Huyton. Also in the small cart was a woman from the agent's office to take notes.

As they approached the outskirts of the town, they were delayed by sheep being driven along the road into the market in the centre of the settlement. Sitting in the sun in the open top vehicle, Alicia was very content to follow the slow moving sheep into the High Street.

The White Harte Hotel was a tall modern building situated at the end of a row of terraced stone built cottages. It stood on a corner facing the road near the cattle market. They secured their means of transport next to the raised pavement and went inside for refreshments.

As they sat in the sumptuous lounge looking out of the front small paned window, they saw an expensive looking carriage. Its body work coloured in gold's and reds, with a pair of matching white horses being controlled by the driver who sat high to the front of the transport. A smart well-dressed woman was staring out of a side window as it drove past.

Alicia was curious, "Do you know who that is?" she enquired of her companion.

Death for a Starter

"She is the Duchess, she and her family live in Huyton Hall, it is a large house - actually we will pass it on the way to the property you are interested in. I suppose in some ways, they will be your neighbour if you decide to go ahead."

"Oh – we will be that close?"

"Not really - the Hall has a lot of land around it and we will be a few miles away. At one time the farm we are going to see was owned by the Duke. It was split into two a long time ago."

"It all sounds very interesting. Shall we go? I am keen to see this place it may be exactly what I am looking for."

Alicia was surprised when she saw the property with a timber frame and a black slate roof. It looked stunning.

"The little road down the side leads to some other cottages." The agent pointed to the left side of the house. Stepping down from the trap he turned and held her hand whilst she dismounted. "The place has been left for some time now. The owner moved out to stay with family. My understanding is they could not cope with what is needed to keep the place working."

They had wandered around the four bedroom house and had gone out into the rear where there was a large yard with some outbuildings.

"Is all this included in the price?"

Death for a Starter

"Yes. And there is a lot more. Where those trees are on the top of the rise in the ground, on the far side is the village of Heady, which this farm is named after. The houses and general store there belongs to the farm" He was pointing with his finger. "I think that is where most of the farm hands live. I assume you will be employing them?"

She laughed, "Hold on! I will have to get my head around all the other things before we start to think about that. How many acres did you say there were?"

"I think it is about eight or maybe nine thousand. The exact amount is on the deeds back in the office."

Alicia had no idea what that amount of ground looked like but it sounded a lot to her. "Have we got time to go and see this village now?"

Removing a watch from his pocket, he said "Yes I think so. We don't have to come back this way; there is another road which will take us back to my office." They started to walk back to their transport and as they drove down the lane beside the house, he pointed out the row of detached cottages all with stone walls to their fronts. "I don't think they have been lived in for a long time, but I am sure you will find a use for them"

A little time later, they finally arrived at the small village, having passed fields on their way with men working in them. As they drove down the one and only road, they saw to each side a variety of houses - most built of the dark stone so

Death for a Starter

common in the area. The agent pointed to a detached property with double doors to the front. "That is the Smithy – my understanding is that he looks after the horses on the farm re-shoeing – that sort of thing. Just a bit further down is the small store."

Alicia was overwhelmed and said very little on the way back to the agents office, deep in thought, thinking *'could they take on a place that size and make it work?'*

She asked "The town of Huyton that is separate – but the village Heady is part of the farm. Is there an income from those properties?"

"Oh yes...I think it is collected quarterly." He was bending over looking into a drawer retrieving the details of what they had seen that day.

Chapter Seven

London England

It had been at the end of the Civil War in England when Royalty was returned to the Throne of England, Scotland and Ireland. Charles II was crowned King after the defeat of Oliver Cromwell and his Roundheads. It was Cromwell who had been one of the signatures on the document that lead to the execution of the King's father, Charles I in 1649.

The new King had been smuggled into Scotland to lead the revolt against the Roundheads and to restore the throne to its rightful heirs. At the head of this revolt against the parliamentarians was Thomas MacHeady he had led the army to overcome the anti royalist rulers who were opposed to the return of the monarch.

Cromwell, whilst in power had the determination to destroy religions which were not to his liking and who

Death for a Starter

supported Royalty, or those which did not worship in the Protestant and Presbyterian manner. He destroyed the Catholic Church by confiscating their lands. The King being so grateful for the work Thomas MacHeady had organised on his behalf granted vast stretches of the Irish countryside to his benefactor.

It would be fifty years later when once more with the help of MacHeady, the King was successful in battle and for the services he and his kin had given in the support of the Monarch, further lands were granted to the family in the north of England, near the progressive city of Liverpool.

Thomas, although still a strong man, despite his long life, built a beautiful house of a wood frame structure, with a lengthy drive leading through an archway into a courtyard. The house became known by the locals as Huyton Hall, named after the nearby small town. Over time the house was developed further as required by the growing household.

In a period when it took a long time for workmen to travel to the far corners of the land holdings, one of MacHeady's sons built a further farm house, dividing the vast land they owned into two. So as not to confuse the two, they called the second Heady's Farm and part of the family moved into it. The small village was built to house the families of the men needed to make the farm a functioning success.

MacHeady's son had no male heirs to continue the family name and when the two daughters married two brothers named Evens, the family inheritance name changed. The elder

Death for a Starter

of the two sisters lived in Huyton Hall with her husband, whilst the younger one changed the name of Heady into Evens' Farm.

**

To the west of the City of London is an army barracks in Kensington, which is not very far from the Houses of Parliament. Monday morning and the troops, as they did every day at the start of the week, saddled horses and attached the harnesses to cannons on steel wheels. It was one of those days when the weather is not too certain of what it wants to do. The sun would be bright and warm before slipping behind a cloud, only to reappear in all its glory. It was teasing the people as it once again turned off the brightness by hiding once more.

In the barracks an exercise was in progress. The troops were on horses riding up and down the parade ground in configuration pulling the cannons. To the front of the spectacle was Major Curtis Evens, an officer who had bought his commission, which in the eighteen hundreds was not unusual. He was a man from the Liverpool area and came from a very wealthy family owning a vast amount of land in England which they worked creating further wealth. Their workers lived in small communities on the property, in cottages built years before. The Evens family also owned land in Ireland which was rented out as small holdings.

Curtis who was the heir to the families' fortunes was a strong self-willed man. One day when he could not agree with his father over the running of the estate, a disagreement which

Death for a Starter

had been a long running sore, after careful thought he bought a commission as an officer in the Army. Because of his strong family history, whose grandfather had been well thought of in the highest circles of Royalty, the Major was welcomed into the forces and promotion had been rapid.

The troops came to the end of the parade ground and were about to make the turn to repeat the process of practising the drill, when Curtis noticed a private whom he recognised as the Regiments Adjutant runner. Holding his hand up, the Major brought the troops to a halt. The runner told the mounted officer he was required in the offices. The private saluted him and turned away. Curtis dismounted and made his way to see the Adjutant.

In the sparsely furnished office with little material comfort, bare un-curtained windows and bare floor boards, Curtis arrived and saluted his superior. After the formalities were over, the Adjutant said "We have learned of a terrible thing. I am sorry to have to tell you that your father has been murdered whilst doing his duty collecting rents due from farmers in Ireland. I understand that they found his body in a burnt out cottage."

The Major sat down on a chair, his eyes had glazed over. "I would like to take leave of absence. My mother will need my help."

"Major we understand that. I think your home is in Liverpool, where she lives, is that correct? If so I have

Death for a Starter

arranged with the Commanding Officer for you to go up north at this terrible time."

"Mother and Father have an extensive farm in the country outside of the city. Do we know what happened to him?"

"No, I am sorry I don't know, the message is very brief." The adjutant was sorting some paper on his desk. Looking up he said "The latest you can be back here is a week on Friday, after that you will be needed. I hope you can complete your business before then. I'm sorry I cannot give you more time, but as you know the regiment is going to India – I'm sorry but we cannot go without you. Have a comfortable journey they tell me the new train service is very good."

"Thank you Sir. I will be back here as required." Curtis saluted and marched out of the senior officer's room. He quickly packed a case and made his way to the railway station where trains ran regularly to the North - albeit very slowly. The maximum speed at that time was no faster than sixty miles per hour.

Chapter Eight

Near Liverpool England

It was a difficult and long journey for the Major. He had made his way to Paddington station in North London by a horse drawn Honsom cab where the train for the north would depart. He walked along the platform with other travellers who were going in the same direction, doffing his hat at the ladies dressed in their finery and headed for the first class part of the train.

The compartment in the carriage was comfortable with its braid covered sprung seating, and very separate from the part of the train which said 'Ladies only' or the third class part with wooden seats. As the train finally arrived in Manchester he had to change on to another service before

Death for a Starter

finally arriving at Liverpool, where he hired a horse for the final part of the journey to his childhood home.

He arrived at the gate and looked fondly at the house which he knew in every detail. It had little nooks and hiding places where as a child he used to play hide and seek and other games, with his brother.

By the front gate was one of the field workers, whom he remembered from the time he was a child, but could not recall his name. He was doing some work tidying up the front of the property. Curtis was about to dismount when the worker spoke. "If you are looking for madam, she has moved out."

"Oh! He paused - he was stunned. "What are you talking about and anyway when would that have been?"

"I think it was about a week ago now Sir. We are told she has gone to stay with relatives. I think she said she would be staying at her sisters up at the Hall - some other people are coming to live here."

"What do you mean...some other people are coming to live here - are you sure? Mother would never leave this house- it has been in the family for years. What is this nonsense of someone else living here?"

"Oh it is right Sir. They were here just the other day, looking round, young family, I think they were Scottish but could have been Irish – can't tell the difference if you ask me. Their name was something like Carton or Corman...something like that. Do you know them Sir?"

Death for a Starter

"Thank you, then it is pointless me going in."

"Yes sir, there is nobody in and they have fixed the doors so you can't open them."

Curtis was fuming. Why hadn't he been told? He violently tugged on the reins, the horse responded and turned, he steered it out of the gate and with the horse in a gallop, rode it fast kicking up dust as he hurtled through the main street of Heady, turning many a head. He pushed the horse, thinking *that maybe it was not too late if the sale had not been finalized.*

Huyton Hall came into view as he breasted a hill, he looked at it's beauty as the sun glinted on its facade. With it was a large acreage of the countryside and when the old man had passed on, he had divided the property into two and left it to his very spoilt daughters, which were his only children, having half of the estate each. The eldest being blessed with the grander property of the Hall, whilst the younger had been given the lesser of the two properties.

The horse had white sweat marks around its neck and on its flanks as Curtis rode fast through the gates, up the long drive and on into the courtyard, where a stable hand held the head of the animal while he dismounted.

He strode into the house calling for his mother. One of the servants directed him to the morning room. She was sitting in a brocade chair listening to her sister playing a melody on a highly polished grand piano near the large bay window; the

Death for a Starter

remainder of the room was lavishly furnished. She stayed seated while he bent over and kissed her on the cheek.

"Hello son. Are you going to say hello to your Aunt?" Curtis nodded to her and she nodded in return whilst continuing caressing the key board with her immaculate red painted nails on her fingers.

His mother picked up and rang, a small silver bell from a side table by her chair. A maid appeared at a door asking "Yes, Mam?" After which she immediately disappeared to go and do her mistress bidding for the afternoon tea. "So you got my letter. I am glad you have come there are a lot of things to sort out and papers to sign."

"Mother I have not had a letter from you. The Army told me what is going on and now I find you have sold the farm – which is, or at least was, my home and my inheritance - would you please tell me what this nonsense is about selling our house? I would also remind you it is not something even you can do without what appears to be my decision, now that father has gone."

"Yes, I have got rid of it. I cannot cope with the farm any longer. Your father has been away chasing debts – a lot of money owed to us by the Irish – and I have been trying to control things with the help of that numbskull who is supposed to be managing – he could not manage anything - how your Father ever came to employ him I do not know. For certain your Father could not see he was totally hopeless."

Death for a Starter

Curtis was taken aback by the force of her words. "But why sell the farm and our home? Anyway you cannot do it without my permission." He threw his hat onto a chair and started to remove his coat.

"What else am I to do? You are away in the army for the next twenty odd years – your Father is dead murdered by heathens they call the Irish. Your sister and brother have gone off to a place they call America because they say life is better over there…Tell me what am I supposed to…Oh never mind it is too late the farm has gone, and now that my sister has lost her husband who's died of some infernal disease, it makes sense for us to live together and keep each other company." She paused looking at her sister who was nodding her head. "Well! How long are you here for?"

"I have just told you mother .You cannot do it without my permission. So it is not too late."

"No! It is too late. I have taken their money and I will not have the family name dragged in the mud because you want to change things and have your own way."

Curtis had always found it difficult to argue with his very dominant mother. She asked him again, "How long are you here for?" He knew he was beaten, he was duty bound to leave with his regiment. There was not the time to enter into a lengthy discussion to try and change her mind. If he stayed here to try and reverse her decision, then the Army would arrest him and he would find himself in front of a court.

Death for a Starter

"In a few days I must be back in London in fact by next Friday. It is not easy travelling this far north, but of course when they complete a direct railway line in a few years' time it will be a lot easier." He thought to himself '*why did I say that*' "I leave for India shortly, and that is why I must return London...what happened to Father?"

"I told you he was murdered whilst collecting rents which are owed to us. We are told they think he was stabbed but nobody is too certain, and then he was left in a building which they burnt down."

"Do they know who was responsible? Anyway how are the rents being collected now on the property we own in Ireland?"

"They tell us it was a family by the name of O'Dowd – they have disappeared – but we understand the army and the police are looking for them. As far as the rents go, I have left it up to the Land Agent. Anyway it was his job in the first place – why your Father got involved I do not know." She was shaking her head, "But it is worse – there is a farm near Dublin which he had wanted to sell for some time and on this trip he had collected the money from the sale, so it was not just rent money he had on him but also the other money from selling the other property."

Curtis was stunned, "How much?"

"Curtis you must understand me! I do not want to go back there it has too many memories - I am tired, I have got no

Death for a Starter

family except my sister, so do what I ask and tomorrow go and sign the papers. The solicitor will tell you what is involved and how much money they have stolen from us. You could also go and see the police to see what they are doing about it – but I do not think it is very much."

"The police are useless - they have too many problems and other villains to cope with to be efficient. It is a pity that I am committed to going away." He paused looking at the two well-dressed ladies, when his mother was in this sort of mood, he knew it was useless to argue with her, and if he did it would take a long time to resolve.

"What we need is someone we can trust to find the culprits who did this deed. There is a firm in London, they call themselves private detectives – I do not know what they charge but I think we should employ them to find these people who killed and stole from my Father. I do not know if such people work out of Liverpool"

Curtis's mother sipped her tea and shrugged her shoulders. If that is what her son wanted then she would not stop him and she would let him organise it. As far as she was concerned she had sold the farm and with the money she had, she had no worries, also living with her sister she had company and nowhere near the daily cost of running her own home.

The next day Curtis rode into the city to find a private investigator and when he arrived he signed some papers to transfer the property to the new owners, after which he visited the police.

He had read about private detectives whilst in London and knew there were establishments which operated there, he as convinced he would find someone who operated in that capacity in Liverpool.

Chapter Nine

After searching the streets of the city and enquiring of shop owners, Curtis finally went into one of the many coffee houses to make enquiries amongst the patrons, to try and find a private detective. In one of the houses was an elderly gentleman with a white beard, he was sitting by a large fireplace with a roaring fire. Held between his teeth was a thick white clay pipe with grey smoke dwindling out of it. He removed it and knocked the ash from it before he spoke "It's my boy you want." Having said his piece, he studied the pipe and seemingly being satisfied with it, put it back into his mouth.

Curtis looked in his direction, not certain if the person sitting by the fire studying the flickering flames from the layer

Death for a Starter

of burning logs in the grate had spoken. "Excuse me Sir – did you say something?"

Removing the pipe again, "Of course I said something - I told you it's my boy you want."

"Does he work as a detective?"

"What have I been saying?"

"Where would I find your – err boy?"

The old man dragged the pipe from his mouth again and with a sigh pointed, "He is sitting over there in the corner, talking to those two lads. Anyway what would a soldier want with him?"

"That is why I want to speak to a private detective - because it is private."

"Oh please yourself. You had better go over to him before he leaves."

"Could you tell me his name – please?"

"Of course it is Harley – do you want the rest of it?"

"No Harley will do, if need be he will tell me the rest. Thank you."

Curtis made his way across the room, squeezing past people sitting at tables reading or discussing the news and other events. Reaching the far corner, he made straight for the

Death for a Starter

table that had been indicated to him, where three people were deep in conversation. They stopped when he got to the table.

"Excuse me but I am looking for Harley?"

The bald headed portly man was wearing a fashionable suit complete with a buttoned waistcoat. In his hand was a jug of beer, whilst the others were holding some papers. With a straight face he slowly looked Curtis up and down, and when his eyes finally settled he looked into Curtis's brown eyes he said "And who is asking for Harley?"

At this stage he was not ready to give his surname and said "My name is Curtis, is there somewhere we can talk in private?" As he said it he was looking at the other two men sitting at the table.

Harley smiled taking a sip of his beer before saying "Of course we can" nodding to the two others he was sitting with. "But first let me finish my business here. If you could find yourself a table, with some privacy I'll be with you shortly."

Another half an hour was to pass and he was getting impatient. Curtis had spent the time looking at one of the news broadsheets, which were delivered to the building on a daily basis so as to keep the patrons up to date with the latest news and events.

Eventually Harley pulled up a chair. He was now wearing a bowler hat. As he sat down he apologised for keeping him waiting. "So Curtis what can I do for you - oh I

Death for a Starter

like to start off on the right foot so I must ask is that your real name?"

The Major was taken back and did not like the question, thinking to himself *'Would an officer and a gentleman deceive someone with a false name?* "Yes Sir of course it is – Major Curtis Evens." He held his hand out and the newcomer shook it with a strong grip.

"So what service can I offer the Major?"

"But first let us talk about you. Who are you and what experience in detective work do you have. And of course cost and I am assuming you work full time at what you do?"

"That is quite a few questions – but let's deal with the cost first, which would depend on what you want me to do and how long it would take and other items like expenses. Before I answer the other questions, you are related, and I guess, son of the land agent who was recently murdered in Ireland. As I remember he was killed and left in a house which was then set on fire. The killers have since vanished and you would like someone to find them. That is because to the police in England they think it is an Irish problem, and the Irish have not got the resources to follow it up with all that is happening in their fair but muddy land. Am I right?"

Curtis smiled "I guess you know what you are doing, and you are right, I am the son."

"Would that be the only son?"

Death for a Starter

"Yes...and no. My brother has emigrated to America. How soon could you get started? I am committed to go abroad with my Regiment in a little while, in fact Friday week."

"I have to finish what I am doing, which is only going to take another few days, it is nothing complicated. Also I magine what you are asking me to do is going to take quite some time. But I guess you are not in a rush. For instance to find the person or people responsible I will need to go to Ireland and start where the crime was committed. I will need to report back to you at intervals when I have some progress – how am I going to do that if you are in India - and how am I going to get paid?"

"It will have to be through the Post Office's packet system, it will take some time to reach me and of course the reply will have to be the same way. But as you say there is no hurry, and I feel certain however long it takes, you will find the people who killed my Father. As for the payment, I will instruct my mother on that, she is living at the Huyton Hall"

After some further discussion they agreed on cost and after exchanging addresses and other details they parted company.

Chapter Ten

*Alici*a was taken aback on the day she moved in with her two children, at the size of the property that she had bought. She loved her new home and it reminded her in lots of ways, of the house she had been brought up in by her parents. This was before the English, under various land acts started to parcel Ireland into small pieces of no more than a few acres, and the Irish had to rent small holdings, which previously they had owned.

Patrick was astonished at the amount of farm machinery that was included with the workings of the farm. He had never seen anything like it, especially the ploughs pulled by two large Shire horses. He toured the farm asking questions of the workers of how things were used and spent the evening in a happy frame of mind planning the changes he wanted to make.

Patrick was still young and with little experience of the work, but over time he took over the running of the farm. In an age when the average life of a man who had toiled since he was five or six years old, was the mid-twenties, it was not unusual for a youthful person to undertake the work that Alicia's son had committed himself to.

The farm hands quickly came to recognise him and his abilities to organise and to have the farm running efficiently. It was not long before Patrick decided that they should sell the

Death for a Starter

farm's produce direct to the public as that way they could make more money, so he set out to find suitable premises to open a greengrocers shop. Whilst doing so he realised that it was simpler to open a market stall in any or all of the frequent markets, open air and enclosed in and around the city.

Whilst Alicia was happy with her new surroundings, she had a deep down fear that sooner or later the police would come knocking at the door to arrest her. In her mind she kept going over the events and the lengths she had gone to, to protect her family and could not see how anyone could find them. She also wondered what event had taken place for the owner of the property to want to leave such a beautiful place, which generated so much money by not only selling the food it produced but the rental income from the properties they owned.

As time went by, she tried to relax a little as she watched her son take control and how the workforce followed his every word and hence the estate, which Patrick called it, continued to grow and to become more profitable. But she was full of guilt at what she had done back in Ireland and on numerous occasions had sought solace in the church in Huyton.

The church became very important in Alicia's life and she insisted the family went on a regular basis. From time to time the Priest would hold small meetings where his flock could get together in less formal circumstances. She became very friendly with a couple whose daughter Victoria was a bright girl and had recently finished school.

Death for a Starter

On one occasion she noticed her son Patrick and Victoria were busy in conversation as they sat at the same table together. Following that occasion it was not unusual to see them talking or walking together when the meeting broke up.

Alicia liked Victoria's parents. They were always smartly dressed and in some ways they reminded her of her own parents, straight laced, honest and never a word that could be construed of anything offensive.

It was many months later when Patrick asked his mother if they could be invited to their home for afternoon tea. After which she was pleased to see the closeness grow between the two and after a while they were inseparable. Their church wedding the following year was celebrated by all. But deep down Alicia could not put the horror of how they had arrived in Liverpool out of her mind. Each new day and nothing heard from the authorities was a blessing to her; but she knew the fear would never leave her.

The nightmares were increasing, she was a wreck from not sleeping properly and getting bad tempered because of it. One day it occurred to her if she went to the police she could bring the nightmares to a stop. The other advantage of taking such a step was that Patrick would be able to keep the farm as she would not involve him in her confession. The night-times were the worst. Alicia did not want to go to bed as she was frightened of the horrors which would come into her head as soon as she was asleep. On occasion she would wake up screaming and the family would rush into the room,

Death for a Starter

because of the noise she was making, and after consoling her, left her to her nightmares which would start all over again. But she did not have the courage to go to the authorities.

Chapter Eleven

In a little Hamlet near Tullamore, a tall portly man wearing a bowler hat driving a horse drawn rig coaxed the animal over the rough ground, which the locals called a road. He approached what used to be the O'Dowd's farm of just a few acres. He noticed that the little stone cottage had a new thatched roof, but evidence of the fire still existed with the smoke blackened walls.

In the field there were two people at work. He called to them - "Do you mind if I look around?"

The man, fearing it was someone from the Land Agent said "Who are you and what do you want?"

"No trouble. I am a detective and I have been asked to look into events that happened here some time ago. I assure you it has nothing to do with your good selves."

Death for a Starter

"Oh aye. We have heard about the goings on here, it was before our time. When we arrived we heard about it, but I think you will learn a lot more if you go to that cottage over there, they were here that night." As he was speaking he was pointing to a cottage in the distance.

Harley thanked them, but before leaving he walked around if only to get the feel of the place. He then got into the carriage and made his way to where he had been directed.

He was disappointed as the elderly couple knew very little, and whilst they were happy to tell him in detail of their involvement of that terrible night's event, they were not much help, although they did make him an offer of a white cow so that he could return it to its owner, which he declined. They were also able to give him a detailed picture of what the family looked like.

As he was about to leave they followed him to his vehicle. She was still speaking as he got into his carriage, "They were regular church people, as it is such a long walk for them, and we would take them in the cart."

"Where would that be?"

"In Tullamore" - she pointed to a track leading away from their home. "If you travel along there you will come to the road which will take you to the town, I am sure the Priest there will be able to help you."

Harley followed the old lady's instructions and a little while later drove over the stone bridge across the River

Death for a Starter

Offaly, from where he could see the steeple of the church near to the centre of the town.

The Priest greeted him as if he was a long lost brother. He had just returned from his morning visits. As he entered the church he was brushing his white hair back over his shoulders.

"Hello my son, you look tired after your travels - perhaps you would like some refreshment?"

"Thank you Father if you would be so kind."

"Let me organise something for you and then we can talk."

A short time later after some water and a slice of local brack (Irish cake) Harley said "That was delicious and most welcome."

"It is obvious you are not from these parts, my guess would be England somewhere around Liverpool? Would I be correct?"

"Perfect. I am here on behalf of clients who are looking for a family who may have passed this way."

"I am intrigued, and of course we do have many people looking for shelter or help of some kind." The Priest was not the type of person to give information freely and sat looking at his guest with blue steely eyes which had seen most things and understood the way people reacted. But on this occasion there was no reaction.

Death for a Starter

"Yes that is my understanding, you must have many strangers looking for assistance, and then again my guess would be you must have members of your flock looking for help."

The holy man nodded his head, once more brushing his white hair away from his face as he remained silent.

Harley was finding it hard work and realised if he was going to get any information from the elderly man sitting opposite him, he would have to be very careful. He continued "Some time ago a cottage caught fire and burnt down. Actually I have just come from there. It was thought the family perished in the fire but I have received information that was not the case and that they have vanished. Could they have come to the church for help as I understand they visited here on a regular basis?"

The Priest was smiling when he asked "You are referring to the O'Dowd's?"

"That is my understanding of their name. Did they come to you for help, Father? Because my knowledge is they had very little in the way of money so they must have received help from someone."

The man of the church was feeling uncomfortable. He also knew they had had plenty of cash with them, but he felt reluctant to part with that information. "They did come here. It was late at night and they explained that their cottage had caught fire and they had nowhere to go. I have a limited

Death for a Starter

amount of funds to help people in trouble. They stayed a little while and then they left. I was worried about the husband he had a terrible cough, which was another reason for wishing to help them; actually I went into the village to get him a mixture to help ease his coughing."

"Do you know where they went to Father?"

"That I am not prepared to say. I have a duty to members of my Parish, what I can tell you is they left after being helped by the church."

Harley knew when he was not going to get any more information, but he continued to try but after a little while he gave up. Thanking the Father he took his leave. Knowing as he left the church - here in this Irish community, someone knew what happened to the O'Dowd's.

Walking through the streets, he came across a few people whom he asked if they knew anything about the O'Dowd family. In his mind he was not too certain that they did not go any further and had settled in this charming Irish town. He thought he would stay a few days to see what he could find. But first he would have to find a stable to look after his horse and rig. After which he had to find somewhere to sleep.

The following day it did not take too long to find out what had happened to the O'Dowd's. It had been common gossip at the time when it had happened. Harley started to ask questions around the village to see if anyone had seen the

Death for a Starter

family. After a while he was told in detail of where they went, also a lot of different opinions of why. One lady remarking "With the cough he had, he was not long for this world." Retrieving his horse and carriage he made his way to the canal and the barges.

On reaching the canal stop, he had a problem in deciding which way they would have gone - towards Dublin or further inland. After thinking for a while trying to come to a decision, he finally made up his mind and made the turn for Dublin.

It took a few days to reach Robertstown. Some of the delay in his journey was caused by the frequent stops asking after the O'Dowd's and if they had been seen. When he finally reached the overnight barge stop, Ross the local constable was more than happy to tell him in detail of the man who had a bad cough and the family, adding "I knew there was something very bad about them."

Finally he reached Dublin, where Harley found a bed for the night and decided he would try and work out what to do from there. First he penned a letter to Curtis informing him of his findings so far - stressing the difficulty of finding someone in the city but emphasising that they could have gone further and emigrated.

The next day after some thought as to where they would have gone, he remembered the Priest in Tullamore – if they went to the church for help once perhaps they have done it again. He made up his mind what his task for the next few days would be - to visit every church in Dublin and the surrounding area. Maybe he would get lucky.

Chapter Twelve

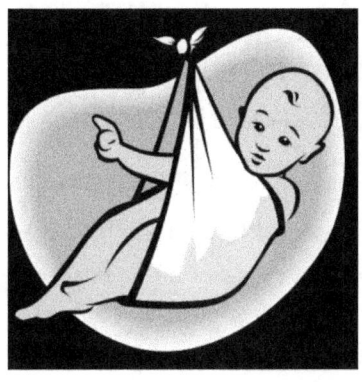

Alicia was delighted when her first grandchild was born. Patrick had married Victoria - a girl whom he had met at their church gatherings. She was just twelve, the legal age at that time for a female to be wed and which had been the previous year.

She gathered up her first grandchild, who was swathed in a soft white knitted shawl. Gently rocking him in her arms as she smoothly sat down in an arm chair near to the window. The bright light reflecting from the glazed window was shining on the baby's face, which had a grin on it as it looked up. The boy's grandmother was smiling back, at this new person in their lives.

"What are we going to call him?" Grandmother asked.

Death for a Starter

"How about a nice English name like Robert and then Reuben – I thought we should include father's name in memory of him" the proud Dad replied.

Alicia said "Yes I like that as we are living in England, Robert is a nice English name, and your Father would have been proud of his second name."

It was a double joyful occasion for the family on that day. By coincidence, Florence, who had been very busy helping in the development of the business, married John - who was a little younger than Patrick. The newly married couple moved into their own cottage which belonged to the Cormack Farm, leaving Patrick and his bride and baby Robert in the original house with their mother.

John had been employed by Patrick in the family business organising delivery of their produce to the company's outlets. The arable and cattle farm which Alicia had purchased, by diligent hard work and foresight, had developed into a thriving business. In a time of questionable food supplies, Cormack's name as a purveyor of fresh food had become well known. As a result it had expanded rapidly, much of it down to Patrick's determination, who had been certain in the early days that by having their own retail shops they could sell direct to the public, therefore making more profit on each item.

The ex-Mrs O'Dowd was trying very hard to put the depressions caused by her fears behind her. Alicia continued helping around the farm and also the joy of looking after her

Death for a Starter

Grandchild, nursing him and trying to amuse him when he was upset.

Despite the arrival of the new family member, Alicia felt more and more down. All the family was remarking on it and wondering what was wrong with her. Frequently Alicia would suddenly put on a coat and leave the house to go for long walks; always deep in thought wondering what action she should take to protect the family. On other occasions she would feel better -thinking to herself '*surely after all this time they would have found her and taken some action.*' But the deep dark horrors would quickly return and she would feel herself falling into a deep chasm of her own thoughts.

One night, she was at peace, as Reuben came in to comfort her - she could see him as if he was alive and was real, standing by the bed. He was beckoning to her to join him and put her mind to rest.

The following morning the vision was fresh on her mind and whilst talking to the family she told them she was going to see their father. They looked at each other in surprise for they all knew what had happened to him. They tried to take no notice, but Patrick was concerned about his mother's health. Shrugging it off, he was thinking that perhaps she had meant the Priest.

The dreams continued. Sometimes Alicia would wake up smiling, at other times the burden on her mind was too great and she would be found by the children kneeling by the bed crying with her hands together praying.

Death for a Starter

On one very cold morning she told everyone she was going to Church to see Reuben. Her kin were at their wits end not knowing what to do, but as she frequently went to church, they thought it would help her and did not put up an argument or try to stop their mother.

Chapter Thirteen

Harley was disappointed. He had visited all the churches and holy places in Dublin but to no avail. He had checked the immigration offices and again drawn a blank - no one had heard of the O'Dowd's. He knew he was wasting his time, they must have gone elsewhere. He once more penned a letter to the Major explaining he was moving on to continue the search for the people that had murdered his father, starting in Liverpool.

The letters Harley was sending to the Major took a long time to reach the officer who was with his unit in India; mail went by ship and had to go round South Africa to get to the Asian Continent. The private detective knew this and could only continue his search following his original instructions until he heard from his client.

By now a long time had passed since the O'Dowd's had vanished and Harley knew the chances of finding them was getting slimmer as each day passed. He joined the scrum

83

Death for a Starter

for the steam driven paddle wheeled ferry, sailing shortly to Liverpool. He got on board, and was aware that this was just one of many ships that crossed the Irish sea. Nevertheless he thought it was worth looking around asking questions of the sailing staff. If the answer was negative, then he would know the chances were that they did not sail on this vessel.

The evening progressed with the boat rolling in the swell of the lively waters of the crossing, the engine thumping below deck in a noisy rhythm setting the fixtures rattling and vibrating in time to its ear-splitting pulsation.

Harley lolled on one of the many benches around the midnight hour. He was trying to sleep but the noise and the movement of the ferry only allowed him to doze at irregular intervals. Unexpectedly somebody in a scruffy seaman's uniform was standing in front of him. At first, only half awake, he was a little concerned.

"You have been asking questions about some passengers?"

"Is that a problem?"

"No - no problem. I may know something and if you are asking - it must have a value."

"Tell me what you know and if it's worth anything then I will pay you."

Death for a Starter

"Let me put it this way – I know the family you are asking about, they were on this boat quite some time ago. I do remember them very clearly and for a guinea I will tell you."

Harley had been in this situation many times before, sometimes he learned something of value, other times it was something he already knew. It was a gamble which he was prepared to take. "Okay – half now and the balance if the information is of any use and not a fairy tale." He held his hand out with ten shillings and sixpence in it knowing it was a lot of money. To the seaman people barely earned that much in a week.

Pointing to another part of the saloon the seaman said "The woman was sitting over there. She had a young girl with her, and there was a boy about twice the girls' age. The boy was wandering around the ship asking question about things. He spoke to me a few times – his father was on deck and it was a very cold night, the man kept coughing, and then he started to spit up blood. It was a little while later he died. And that sir is why I remember it very clearly - because we don't get many people dying on the crossing."

"What happened to him?"

"We don't have facilities for dead people and there is the risk of spreading disease, or whatever he had. It could easily be spread around the other people on the ship, so he was put overboard."

"Are you certain he was dead?"

Death for a Starter

"Oh yeah of course he was, well he wasn't breathing - afterwards I came down here and told the wife what had happened – well, I think it was his wife. The kid was making a fuss and crying and when I left them he was sitting next to the woman. Now that must be worth the rest of the money." Harley was very happy with the information also knowing it was true, as it fitted in with what he had already been told. He thanked the sailor and fishing in his purse paid him the balance of the money. He took a notebook out of his pocket and made a note in the expenses column.

**

Alicia had her own pony and trap which she drove herself. It had been included in the deal when she had bought the farm and although she drove it, it was one of the stable hands that put the harness on the animal and attached it to the two wheeled personal transport.

In front of the church in Huyton, was a gravel drive that the little horse was used to turning into. Here it knew it would be able to graze on the fresh grass on either side whilst it waited for her to return.

Alicia left the pony to its own devices, her mind in a whirl. The night before she had seen Reuben and had spoken to him, she could hear his soft words - words impressed on her memory from the days they were together. At one stage she was stroking his cheek and he was smiling just like he did all those years ago when they had first met. Once more he was enticing Alicia to join him so they could be together again.

Death for a Starter

When she walked into the cool quiet comfort of the church, she was disappointed to find that the Priest was not in attendance. Taking Reuben's hand, for she was certain it existed; she knelt at a pew and prayed. After a while she spoke to her husband, "We will leave and go to the church in Liverpool where I first stayed when we came here from Ireland." She got up and still holding his hand went out to the buggy where she helped the imaginary husband onto the seats.

She arrived at the church near to the port in Liverpool, leaving the horse and cart to its own devices again, as she entered the church. She saw the priest who she normally saw in Huyton, coming out of the vestry. He was holding a boys hand and talking to him. "We did not find any nits this time but I think we should have another look next week, after choir practice."

He looked up and saw Alicia and seemed embarrassed, he let go of the youngster's hand saying "Run along now and remember what I told you." The boy scampered off.

"Hello, Alicia welcome. What are you doing here and how can I help you?"

"Father I want you to give us your blessing because I am going away with my husband."

"Ho!! Where are you going to?"

Death for a Starter

She turned her head and was looking to her side smiling as she said, "We are going to be together like we used to be. And Father will give us his blessing."

Turning to the minister she continued, "We got parted a long time ago but now we are together again. Would you give us your blessing Father?"

The Priest was looking around the church thinking that Alicia was looking at someone he had not seen. Then he realised that she thought there was a person sitting next to her.

"Of course." He muttered not certain what was happening. "What is your husbands' name?" He knew in his mind, because of her previous visits to him, that his visitor was not well and was having difficulty in coping with reality. Nevertheless he decided to go along with her wishes.

"Of course, silly me, you have never met him - his name is Reuben O'Dowd." As she moved towards a pew, she seemed to be holding someone's hand and leading them. Alicia sat down and as she did so she patted the seat beside her.

The holy man was even more confused "But I thought your name was Cormack?" He then remembered that the Priest he had replaced a few months before, had told him the story of the authorities looking for a family called the O'Dowd's. *'Was there any connection with what the woman had told him.?'*

"Don't be silly Father I have just told you my name."

Death for a Starter

As he had done on many other occasions when she visited the Church, the Priest would offer words of comfort, as he did this time, but found it difficult talking to two people, one of which did not exist. Shortly after, she got up and started walking down the aisle, again as if she was holding someone's hand. For the first time the man of the church saw a smile on her face, as she said "I'll go with Reuben now."

Although he was worried about her, he could not see what he could do and as he turned back from whence she came, he saw that she had left her coat on the back of the seating.

**

Harley was aware of the vessel starting to slow as it approached the dock on the side of the River Mersey; the crowd of travellers were gathering their things and picking up bags preparing to disembark. The private investigator was in no rush and was hanging back behind the crowd looking forward to going into his office to see what had happened whilst he had been away.

Walking down the gangplank from the ship holding on to its side as the walkway swayed in the wind he made his way ashore. In the distance he could see a church spire. Realising it was on his way to his office, he decided he would call in and make a start there to look for the O'Dowd family.

Most of the throng of people were walking away from the boat, whilst others were being met by friends or relatives.

Death for a Starter

A few people were making their way onto the vessel for its return to Ireland, but there were not too many going in that direction, most people were trying to leave that troubled land.

Harley could not help noticing the lady in a green dress with no coat on what was a cold morning; she seemed to be talking to herself and smiling. Arriving at the church he was aware of the pony and trap. By now the animal had pulled the vehicle across to some grass on a fresher plot than the feed beside the road. He noticed the name above the wheel arches 'Evens' - it was a sign which Alicia had been intending to change ever since she had bought the farm. Thinking there must be people in the church who may know where the O'Dowd's were, he went in, but first he must secure the horse. It was someone's negligence not to have done it before.

He was surprised to find nobody else inside the sanctuary. The Priest dressed in a long cassock, heard him walking down the nave and came out to greet him "Hello Father - is someone with you?"

"No my son I am on my own. Why do you ask?"

"There is a pony with a rig attached on the lawn outside, and I expected someone to be here. It had the name of Evens' on the side."

"Oh that silly woman, she's either forgot it or she has gone across the way to the shops – she also left her coat here." The holy man pointed to the article on the rear of one of the pews, as he spoke.

Death for a Starter

Harley could not see how any of this was his business. Shrugging his shoulders very slightly he asked, "My name is Harley I am a private investigator - I'm feeling a little weary as I have just got off the night boat from Ireland. But that has nothing to do with your good self. I have been looking for a family called O'Dowd. Information given to me says they came over here to Liverpool, and I wondered if you have had any dealing with them."

The priest was taken aback and a look of surprise registered on his face which Harley immediately recognised. "The look on your face tells me you know them Father?"

The man of the church was so astonished he was almost in shock. How could these two events of the morning be related? He was standing in the middle of the church with Harley standing in front of him wondering what was happening. Was he being set up for something or was it some form of joke? First one of his flock had arrived who he knew as Alicia Cormack - she pretends to have someone with her who she called O'Dowd, but as far as he could see there was no one there. Now a person he has never met before arrives and says he is looking for the O'Dowd's who as far as he was concerned did not exist. "Well Father?"

"Please give me a minute - for you see son I am a little confused. In all the time I have been in the church I have never known a situation such as we have now. Let me explain. Alicia Cormack comes to me regularly, she has been very upset recently and has been visiting almost daily, and she drives here from the farm she owns a few miles from the town of Huyton. This morning she seemed more relaxed than she has been for many months, and knelt just there where her coat is and prayed." He paused and looked around him and at the roof, clasping his hands in front of him, before continuing

"Then she asked for my blessing - but this is the strange thing she pointed to a person who she said was her husband but there was no one there. Even stranger still I thought I would humour her and went along with what she asked - so I asked her his name and she says 'O'Dowd of course,' and said they are going away together."

It all fell very quickly into Harley's mind "Was she wearing a green dress and no coat?"

"Yes, as I said her coat is here" the Priest said and pointed to it.

Thank you Father. I'll get on my way because I think I know where she is going and I had better be very quick." He turned and walked briskly through the door as he left the church.

Alicia was happily striding down the hill towards where the Irish ferry was moored, the boat waiting for its schedule time for the return sailing. There was a trickle of people making their way to the gangplank where they were paying their fare for the crossing.

She was smiling and laughing, quite oblivious to the stares she was receiving.

Death for a Starter

Behind her, Harley was running trying to catch up with her. He was certain he understood what she was planning, the information concerning her husband running through his head of how he had died on the boat and had been pushed overboard. He could see her in the distance approaching the gangplank.

Reaching the access way to the ferry, she approached it boldly and without stopping she walked up the incline on to the ship, ignoring the cries from behind her demanding the." fare. One of the deck hands stopped what he was doing intent on restraining her. She was saying "I am going to Reuben

The deckhand paused, wondering who Reuben was, but continued going after her. Harley was too far behind to help, although he could see what was happening and watched as Alicia was shouting something. The deckhand was trying to stop her. She turned and kicked the deckhand hard in the shin, he doubled up in pain. She then turned and ran across the deck and threw herself over the side into the fast flowing cold waters of the Mersey, which was heading for the bitterly cold Irish Sea.

There was nothing Harley could do. He turned and out of respect for the Church, he visited the Father and explained the story to him. After which he walked to his office to pen a letter to the Major. He realised he would have to wait a long time before he would receive a reply from the officer. In the meantime he would go to the Huyton Hall and collect his expenses and any other money owed to him.

Chapter Fourteen

Somewhere in India

On the Plains and not very far from the Major's tented camp stood the snow-capped mountains of the Himalayas forming a backdrop to the line of white tents, their flaps rustling in the breeze. It was early in the morning and the crystal clear dew was dropping off the fly sheets and the guy ropes, as the sun appeared struggling to rise in the East to create another blistering day.

The Major had risen half an hour earlier, when it was still dark, and was sitting at his portable desk which had an oil lamp hanging above it. In its' flickering soft light he was reading the correspondence that had come by courier the previous day.

Death for a Starter

Amongst the communications from the army was a letter, now many months old in its travelling time from England, as official army post had taken priority. He immediately recognised the hand writing of Harley's second dispatch. Opening the package in trepidation, he read the news of the private detective's findings, and was delighted to learn of what had happened, but saddened when he read the husband was dead and she had committed suicide, as he had wanted to deal with them personally.

As Curtis continued to read the findings of the detective he became very hot under the collar, when he realised his mother had sold his inheritance to the very people who had murdered his father. *'God I wish I was not in this forsaken hole'* were his thoughts as he dearly would like to have been back home so he could start proceedings to get his property back.

By now the sun had completed its task and was in full bloom just above the horizon. The Major could hear someone running down the lines of the white bivouac tents each of which slept two men, all of which were up and about - getting ready for the day's events. Behind the tents stood the troops horses who had spent the night in a makeshift corral, watched over by two guards.

The officer could hear the footsteps getting closer to him. His tent was larger than standard issue as it was needed for the administration work of commanding the unit which he needed to undertake. He was hoping it was not a message for him which would mean his troop taking some form of action,

Death for a Starter

as he wanted to finish the letter he had started with further instruction for Harley.

It was the troop's sergeant who appeared at the unsecured flap to the front of the tent. He had received information passed to the army that the rebels were planning a big uprising and were gathering in the bush to collate their forces, before charging into the township to destroy and capture any English they could find. He saluted and said, "Sir, we have just received a report the rebels are forming in the hills the other side of the town."

Major Curtis Evens had been patrolling with his unit for the past ten days, making camp in suitable locations in the early evening before darkness fell. Their orders were to search out the trouble makers who were trying to form a political party to question the English Rule. In doing so they had been causing trouble amongst the working people at places of production and in some cases burning down the tea plantations, the produce of which was destined for the United Kingdom.

The Major gave orders to his junior to secure the camp and prepare to be on the move to confront the group. The men of the unit hurriedly retrieved their saddles and other kits, mounting the horses as they did so. Some, in their haste, were still doing up buttons on their uniforms. Shortly after, they were riding across the open plains towards the hills where the information given to them had said the enemy were forming.

Death for a Starter

Curtis was in front of his troops on a beautiful white stallion. In the distance he could see a band of men who seemed to be disorganised as they were milling around. He thought *while they are in that state it is time to go.* He stood up in the stirrups and holding his arm up he encouraged his men to charge as he flung his arm forward.

With a thunder of the hooves the group picked up speed and were charging up the incline. The troop's standard bearer was riding very close to Curtis, the pendant on a lance fluttering in the breeze with the speed of his mount.

On the hill the rebels were trying to reform, there seemed to be no real procedure in what they were doing and it was obvious they had been taken by surprise. The soldiers were getting closer very fast. The revolutionaries were splitting into groups, one of which had moved to one side from which the occasional white puff of a gunshot could be seen which was being aimed at the advancing uniformed men.

Another group of the warriors they were up against, had formed a little further to the right of the main body of men. The Major then saw they were well prepared with defences to hide behind and in a position to send a hail of bullets in their direction. He also realised they had split into two, and if he kept his men riding in the direction they were heading, they would be in a pincer being attacked from two sides.

As they travelled further up the incline, the ground was not as firm as the level, with gulley's and loose stones on

Death for a Starter

the surface. Some of the horses were stumbling but the commanding officer knew that if they stopped or slowed their advance, the chance of success was slim. He turned the group to the larger of the rebel gang; the gun fire from them was thickening - the white smoke almost continuous. To his left he saw the standard bearer fall, the pendant being quickly picked up by a following rider. Curtis was urging his men on. He died charging - the bullet hitting him in the chest. His horse was also hit, causing the animal to stumble, throwing the dead Major over its head, where he rolled on the ground as the rest of the platoon thundered past.

Back in the Majors' tent a new sheet of paper lay on his desk, its heading read "Dear Harley" - and no more. A lot later when the remains of the troop returned, an orderly screwed it up and destroyed it. The soldier then gathered up the personal effects of his Commanding Officer including the letters he had received from Harley, and packed them in the Major's sea trunk. After securing the lid, he wrote out a label addressing it to 'The Evens Farm, Near Liverpool, England. The trunk was eventually collected and the Army put it into their system for it to be transferred back to England and the address as written on the sticker.

**

When Victoria's mother in law Alicia died, she was pleased, not at the loss of someone she loved, although with some tension, but now she could reorganise the house to her own requirements. No longer would there be the terrible silence between them when they were alone. She was thrilled

Death for a Starter

with the new home she had created, each room decorated and refurnished. While the work was being carried out they had lived in one of the cottages on the estate. In a wifely way the farm house was made into a stunning home of the time, with all of the latest features.

Patrick had been too busy with the running of the business, to be involved in their new home, so on the day they had planned to move in, Victoria was excited and keen to show her husband where they were going to live. She took his hand and guided him around the rooms, her excitement was infectious and one thing led to another especially when they got to the newly decorated and furnished bedroom. It was a little over nine months later that Margaret was born.

Victoria was furious, so she made a decision. In one part of the refurbished house was an unused room, and on his return home one evening he discovered his clothes and other things had been moved into it, including a bed.

Chapter Fifteen

Liverpool England

Harley had no idea how long it would take for a letter to reach his client, although he was a little surprised that he had not had a reply from his first and earlier letters. Although, what he did not know was that one was on the way to congratulate him on his efforts so far. As he had not received it, he was in a quandry what decision to make about the case.

It appeared to him that he was in a unique position, knowing what he knew about the ownership of the Evens Farm. He had been putting off going to Huyton Hall to collect what was owing to him whilst he was waiting to hear from Curtis. But now he was wondering if something had happened to him and he was not in a position to reply. Making a decision, he decided he could not put off the visit any longer. The following day he arrived at the gates to the magnificent property and asked to see Mrs Evens. After a bit of confusion over which one of the ladies he wanted to see, he was finally shown into a very comfortable sitting room.

Death for a Starter

He was aware that from this very house, the man who had controlled the whole area had once lived. A man so powerful the King of the time, in return for his loyalty and help in raising an army to protect the monarchy, had bequeathed the land to him. But now, what had been a beautiful property was in decline through lack of management and relatives that did not have the same desire or drive as the original owner.

The situation which had developed after the murder of the father of the house and the trail of events he had uncovered. He could only see a vast sum of money for himself, especially if the Mrs Evens was not interested and had sold the farm on because she could not be bothered to run it. He realised that he was the only person who knew what had happened, and he thought he would keep it to himself until he had heard from the Major, with no doubt further instructions.

"More money young man - and what is this for?" He could see that Mrs Evens was not in a very good mood.

"For work carried out and agreed by the Major - there are also some expenses in the figure. Would you like to go through them with me?"

"I would not like to do anything with you - and I do not see why I should pay such an enormous sum of money" she said in a haughty way.

"I understand your feelings Madam, as you were not party to mine and the Major's agreement. He has been sent the figure and no doubt if he disagrees with it then he would have been in touch."

"So tell me what you have been doing to earn…as you say 'the figures' you are putting before me?"

"I have travelled to Ireland…" He was interrupted.

"Yes, you told me all that last time – and I paid you. I thought that was the end of the matter?" She was staring at him as he stood opposite her, as she had not offered him the facility to sit down.

"It was up to that time, but since then I have carried on my investigations as instructed by your son, trying to find the people that killed your husband. This has taken up a lot of my time, and of course the cost of doing what was required by following my instructions. It has taken a lot of travelling which I have had to carry out in my quest to find the killers…"

"…how do I know what you are telling me is true ... you could have been sitting on your back side all day dreaming imaginary figures to give to me? You certainly have not come up with the killers. If you think you are going to leave here with wads of money in your purse then you had better think again. I am not in a position to know what the arrangement was between you and my son." She was wiping a tear from her eye. "For you see Curtis has been killed in action whilst in India. So Mr…Harley there is not going to be any more money. Please leave now and I do not want to see you again."

Death for a Starter

"I will do that then and I wish a good day to you then Madam." Harley was in shock. He could see no amount of argument would change her mind and he was of the opinion she was too proud to believe she had sold her home to the people that had killed her husband. He turned on his heels, red in the face and holding the tails of his fashionable dark long coat, walked out of the room. He was thinking to himself that he had done the right thing in not telling her the truth of who the villains had been, as now he was in a position to seek recompense from the people occupying the Evens Farm.

**

Eventually the Major's trunk arrived complete with all his personal effects and the communications from Harley explaining what had taken place on that fateful day and after, when his father was killed. He also went on to explain what had happened to the O'Dowd's and how they had used the money they had stolen to buy the farm which used to be his home. Long before Curtis's personal effects had arrived by the roundabout route, Mrs Evens had received news of the death of her son from the Army. The trunk was a tragic reminder of what might have been for her and her family. She left it sealed and ordered one of the servants to store the offending item in the cellar, where it was to stay for many years, lying to one side, gathering dust and cobwebs.

Chapter Sixteen

Patrick, although not a very religious man, insisted they should go to church on Sunday mornings. He was dressed in his Sunday best with a top hat perched on his head and was riding with his wife Victoria and his sister Florence in the farm's shining black four wheeled carriage with a visible mark where the original owners name of 'Headys' had been removed, and "Cormack" replaced it. John was unable to attend as he was busy with work on the farm.

Arriving outside the church he alighted and helped his wife and sister both dressed in their finery to step down from the vehicle through the small door.

As they walked towards the church down the gravel path, Patrick felt, more than knowing, that he was being watched. Suddenly he turned around and noticed a portly man holding a bowler hat in his hand which he had removed before

Death for a Starter

entering the holy place. He had seen the man earlier when they had alighted from the carriage. He felt at the time he had been waiting for them, as he appeared to be taking an interest but he put it down to the gentleman admiring the two ladies in his care.

The three of them sat in their normal pew and waited for the service to start, after which they filed out bidding farewell to the Priest, who was standing in the doorway shaking the congregation's hands and wishing people well, as they walked out into the sunshine.

Patrick had helped his wife into the vehicle first and was helping Florence into the carriage when there was a tap on his shoulder. He half turned to see the man who had been holding the bowler hat in the church, which was now on his head. He was asking him "its Mr O'Dowd isn't it?"

It was an instant shock and he knew his face had registered the wrong expression of a fearful surprise. He recovered quickly "I'm sorry you must have the wrong person, my name is Cormack."

The detective lifted his bowler hat in recognition of the two ladies and said "Oh of course it is Mr Cormack." He said it with a very strong emphasis on the name. "May I take the liberty to come and visit you…shall we say on Tuesday in the afternoon?"

Death for a Starter

Although he did not feel it, Patrick answered, "It will be a pleasure to see you Sir, and may I ask what your business is, also we do not know your name?"

"Everyone calls me Harley. Good day to you, until Tuesday when I will explain everything." Once more he doffed his hat towards the ladies and turned and walked away.

Patrick was feeling a bit stupid as he had not insisted when he asked the man what his business was and why he wanted to visit, but deep in his heart he knew what the man wanted to talk about. Turning, he quickly stepped into the coach and told the driver to move on. As he did so he looked over his shoulder and he could see the man with the bowler hat, who had stopped and was looking at them. He was puzzled and could not help wondering who he was. All the way back to the farm he felt uncomfortable, he knew they had been found out, and was surprised because he had believed, after the suicide of their mother, it would be the end

A few days were to pass, days in which Patrick could not help feeling nervous with a habit of looking down the road to see if any strangers were making their way in their direction. One afternoon while he was working at the table adding up figures, there was a knock on the door. He visibly jumped with fright, opening it only to see a farm hand wanting instructions for some work he was doing. The owner sighed with relief and after managing a few stutters, regained control to answer the farm hands' query.

Death for a Starter

**

On the Tuesday morning when he was to meet the Cormack's that afternoon, Harley had gone to his favourite tavern. He was a widower whose wife had died a few years earlier from one of the deadly diseases that one could so easily pick up from a city whose sanitation was very poor. He had mourned her passing, and although he had been tempted once, when he was introduced to a woman, he had not pursued it as his work was his life, which he thoroughly enjoyed, and the necessary travelling was another reason not to get involved with anyone else.

The tavern was the one place he felt comfortable in. There were friends and business acquaintances, also plenty of women to have fun with. Although some of the characters were unsavoury and no doubt so crooked they would rob their own grandmother. But he did not care as he liked the company, the laughter, and the atmosphere and it was somewhere he could find female company without any strings attached. The women earned their living by the tips they were given by keeping the men happy.

The room was smoky as usual, not only from the numerous pipes being puffed but also the fireplace the chimney of which had not been swept for a long time and was now partly blocked. Every now and then a puff of grey/black smoke escaped into the room.

Harley was holding a jug of ale in one hand, the other stroking the back of the woman who was sitting on his lap.

Death for a Starter

Her coloured full flared skirt had risen up and she was swinging her legs, in time with the soft music coming from a mouth organ one of the men was playing. As he put his beer down on the table to their side, he could see down between her full breasts, as the off the shoulder blouse sagged forward.

"Are we going somewhere for a little bit of fun?" She was smiling at him and kissing him on the cheek as she said it.

"Maybe later I have something I have to do this afternoon."

She pouted, stroking his leg below the knee. "I haven't seen you for so long…and now you are saying 'No' to me." She slid off his lap, pulling her skirt down as she did so. He reached into his coat and took out a wallet from which he extracted some coins. "As I said - later when I get back from what I have to do. And then we will celebrate"

"Aw…I like Celebrations." She kissed him on the cheek as she said.

On the far side of the room, two scruffy looking men were swigging beer and exchanging local gossip, when one of them said, "Did you see that?" He nodded his head in Harley's direction, "The fat slob with the bowler sitting over there talking to Molly. He has just taken a fat wallet out of his pocket."

The other looked in the direction his friend had indicated, "He used to be a Constable, and he is the sod who got my brother put away, all because he nicked a few apples

Death for a Starter

off a cart. They were going to string him up but instead they sent him to one of those penal colonies. I owe him one. I was fond of my little lad but now we will never see him again."

"Well let's do it. No doubt he will cut down through the alley on the way to the stables."

The two of them got up and made their way out of the door.

That afternoon Patrick waited a little tense for their expected visitor. He was finding it difficult to do any work and as the evening approached he knew he was not coming, but was wondering why and what would the man with the bowler do next.

Molly on the other hand had gone back to the tavern and waited for Harley to turn up as promised earlier that day. As the time passed and there was no sign of him, she came to the conclusion that she was wasting her time waiting for him and she should look elsewhere. When one of her old customers approached her Molly agreed to spend some time with him, and give Harley a mouthful of abuse next time she saw him.

To the rear of the tavern, Molly was walking hand in hand with the other gentleman she frequently had a liaison with. They had left the darkly paved street stepping over the gutter to go into an alleyway which would lead them to the stables, where her friend's carriage would be waiting.

Death for a Starter

A street gas light faintly glowed on a cast iron post, which earlier had been lit by the gasman using a small ladder who had reached up to light it. The dim illumination was at the end of the dark walkway throwing a flickering glow creating long shadows in the narrow pathway. There were piles of rubbish which had been discarded and in a corner she saw two wild dogs pulling at something. Molly screamed, one of the animals had a hand in its mouth, and as it pulled at it, an arm appeared. Using his stick, her companion frightened the dogs away. Her friend struck a match so they could see who it was. She recognised him instantly. It was Harley, very white with dried blood at his forehead. She now knew why he had not arrived earlier.

Chapter Seventeen

New York City in Development

Owen Evens had arrived in his new country three years previously, after a flaming row with his father who had expected him to travel around Ireland collecting the rent from the poor tenant farmers. He, with his brother Curtis had seen it as robbing people who were trying to eke out a hard living in an unforgiving land. The brothers took the view that payment for the rent was far too high and not sustainable. The property they were allowing these poor souls to live in, in their view, was disgraceful..

The resultant argument broke up the family, and whilst his brother had bought himself a commission in the British Army, Owen booked passage on the first iron clad passenger ship the SS Great Britain which had been completed

Death for a Starter

a few years before, to cross the Atlantic. Owen had travelled in luxury as a first class passenger with his every whim being seen to - and marvelled in the ship as it sped across the Ocean, arriving at the Castle Garden Depot near Manhattan, with the ever familiar seagulls following behind, swooping on the fish that the great ship had churned up in its wake.

He was surprised at what he found; New York was teaming with Irish people fleeing from their homeland away from the ravages of the continuing famine caused by the failure of the potato crop. Some of the immigrants had crossed the great divide of water from their homeland in questionable craft, confined to a cramped space below decks.

With his English schooling and University background, he quickly found work helping in the design of one of the new railroads which were being constructed at that time, to cross America from East to West. The work he was involved in was the completion of Hoboken Rail Terminal, situated beside the Hudson River, from where the Irish were helping to lay the tracks to spread the railway westwards across the States.

Owen settled down to his new life, quite different from the one he had been used to. The status he had had in England, totally gone and he found that respect came from achievement. This also went for his living accommodation, but in some ways he was enjoying himself finding the work and the people he worked with fascinating.

Death for a Starter

As the weeks and the months passed and although he had written home frequently, neither his mother nor father ever replied. After a while he stopped writing and concentrated on his work, returning home in the evening to the small house he had rented in Manhattan. The invitation to the celebrations of the company's party to celebrate their fifth anniversary was very welcome, but a little disappointing when the planned event turned out to be on a very cold winter's night. Leaving the small house to face the Arctic winds and unable to find a cab, he walked the half a mile or so to reach the venue.

The evening had progressed with speeches and individuals from the management team were slapping each other on their backs and congratulating the success of the railroad they were building. Owen felt left out of the celebration, his English upbringing and reserve was not letting him show the same enthusiasm.

That evening his life was to change. Rose was a slim charming lady, who he had seen briefly in the past working in one of the many offices of the company, and was one of the few women at the celebrations. Now here she was talking to a group a little way from him. He was totally captivated by her beauty, she looked stunning with her long full skirt and shapely top with a row of pearl buttons up to her neck emphasising her slim waist. Whilst he was finding it difficult to take his eyes off her on a few occasions, he would be rewarded when she would look his way and smile.

Death for a Starter

He knew the group of men he was with only because he worked with them. They were standing in a circle, each with a glass in hand, chatting about the work they were doing and how it was progressing. Sean the one Irishman in the group was standing next to Owen - and had been telling Irish jokes all evening. Because of his broad accent, only a few people could understand him.

Suddenly he said "Rose is over there, I've been wondering where she was." He turned and waved to her, she was standing with some of her office colleagues. "Rose come over and join us." He added, "She works in the next room to me. Oh and did you know her father is the big boss?"

She nodded, and after a brief word to her friends, glided over and joined their group sliding herself between Sean and Owen. Their introduction by one of the delegates was a fiery instant, both feeling the magic of the moment. Her perfume wafted over him and their eyes locked together, hers dancing in the flickering lights of the room. He knew instantly it was someone he wanted to see again.

The pair soon became very close and were frequently seen together, even in the office when break time came. He was invited to visit her parents who lived in a beautiful house overlooking the new Central Park which was still under construction, where he was made welcome and it was not long before he became a regular visitor.

There were no clouds that night and a full moon lit up the beautiful clear star clustered sky, creating a perfect night

Death for a Starter

for the young couple as they trotted along in the horse and buggy towards their favourite eatery. It had been a warm day in the latter part of May. Rose and Owen had spent the afternoon celebrating her twenty first birthday, and after a fabulous lunch laid on by her family, they had just been sitting in the sunshine or walking along the banks of the Hudson river lost in each other's thoughts. The meal for the evening had been arranged in a locally well-known restaurant, situated in aged premises in the old part of New York.

The restaurant had not changed over the years, retaining its old attraction, excellent food and service. From the outside the same charm of the building excelled with its Tudor timber construction and plaster inlays – on the inside low ceilings with oak beams crossing from side to side, all dating back to when the first settlers had started to arrive seeking a new life in the United States.

The couple were sitting in one of the dark oak booths with a glazed glass panel to the top, which divided the room into individual private spaces. Owen was holding her hand on the seat beside them, "I try to imagine what my life would have been like if I had not decided to come here."

"You told me you lived in a large house in the country, surely that would have been enough."

"I thought it was at the time. The same safe routine each day…walking around the estate pretending you know what each man is doing…no need to worry about anything as there is a man servant to look after your every whim. Being

115

Death for a Starter

here has changed my view on life. Going out to work in the morning after having got one's own breakfast, which was novel at first. I did not think I would ever get used to it – but funny thing is I enjoy doing it…I'm sorry I am rambling on."

"Of course not – I love listening to you and I want to know all about you."

"You are so different from the women I knew in England. You are more relaxed with no airs or graces – just great company and I am very much in love with you – there is not a moment when I am not thinking of you and at night you occupy all my dreams."

Rose squeezed his hand, "Thank you that is very nice." She had turned her head and was smiling up at him.

I am so pleased I went to the celebration for the fifth anniversary. I nearly didn't because of the snow and there were no cabs about, so I had to walk. If I hadn't done that I may never have got to know you."

Rose tightened her grip on his hand as she replied, "Our paths would have crossed somewhere…anyway you have said that a thousand times"

"If it is that many I must mean it" He was looking into her eyes and smiling as he said it. "I was very jealous when I saw you talking to those other men."

"I came over at the first opportunity, didn't I?" They continued looking and smiling at each other, miles away from the world, which at that moment did not exist. "You are looking nervous - something wrong?"

"No...nothing really – I was just wondering it has been over a year since we first met and..." Owen was looking uncomfortable, taking a deep breathe he picked up her hand and holding it to his lips, "Will you marry me...please?"

Rose was smiling and then gave a little giggle, "Of course I will." She leant forward kissing him on the lips. "But first I think you will need to talk to Daddy."

Owen had always been welcome at the home of Rose's parents, but on the occasion he went there to ask for her hand in marriage, he was feeling uncomfortable and very nervous. Her father, a tall man always dressed immaculately even when relaxing at home, took him into his book lined study. "So young man you want to take my daughter away from me?"

It was not the question Owen had expected, he started to stutter, "No...well yes really."

The older man laughed, "Well it had to happen one day...and what I can ask is what your plans are? You don't want to take her back to your palatial home in England, do you?"

"No sir that is not in my plans. I have grown very fond of America and I want to stay and help in the development of the country. My intention is to buy a house not too far from here

Death for a Starter

– I have funds in England which I intend to transfer here, to be able to do that."

"I see." He sat down behind the large desk that dominated the room and stared at the young man seated in front of him. "I did not know that. I have watched you since you have worked for us and even more so since you have been courting our Rose – so this is no surprise and in some ways I am very happy, but sad as I like seeing her and having her company around the house. Son, I am more than happy for you to marry into our family, and you will be very welcome and have my full support. Shall we go and give the news to the others?"

The wedding between Owen and Rose was the talk of the town and written about in the newspapers as the wedding of the year. It took place twelve months later in a ceremony attended not only by most of their friends and workmates but also the dignitaries of the city. Eighteen months later when their first son Josh was born, he wrote home to his mother telling her the news, although he waited for her reply, none ever came. Another year was to pass when Josh had a sister Clementine – once again he wrote to England but his letters were ignored.

Chapter Eighteen

The late Eighteen Hundreds

The auction in the open market in Huyton was under way, with cattle and sheep in individual pens of steel tubing - the animals all making their own peculiar noises. The buyers and sellers were gathered around, some standing, others leaning on the fences of the pen dividers.

A group were gathered outside the tavern with jugs of ale in their hands, all were listening to the events being played out in front of them. The auctioneer was seated on a raised platform to one side, and was waving a gavel around, as he monitored the bids coming in from the audience for two cattle that were being paraded around the ring in the centre. Overhead the puffy white clouds were being blown across the sky in the brisk breeze, with birds flying around in circles looking for a morsel of food that they could swoop on.

The auctioneer was calling for any more bids, looking around him at the faces to see if one of them would nod to increase the sale price. As there was no response he raised the gavel and brought it down with a bang on the small table in front of him. Shouting "Sold to Mr Wiley" as he did so.

Just behind the auctioneer was the clerk where the buyers went to settle their account. "Wiley" sported a black beard with streaks of grey in it. His felt hat was on one side of his head with his long hair escaping below it as he sauntered over to the table whilst opening the flap on the pouch at his side.

The clerk had already made out the bill of sale using a quill pen, and was drying the ink with a blotter, he handed the paper to him, Wiley said "Who was the seller?"

"You know better than to ask that, but as it happens she does not mind if they are known."

"She – what do you mean she?"

"One of the Cormack's, her name is Florence. I think you will find her in the Tavern – that is where she normally is on sale days."

Wiley felt excited. He had often wondered how he could be acknowledged by the Cormack family. They were well known and had money, perhaps this was the lead to them he had been looking for.

Making his way through the crowd he arrived at the beer house. On the way he had been stuffing tobacco into a wooden pipe with the figure of a ladies face carved into its front. Entering the building he saw Florence at once sitting on her own by the fireplace with skirts splayed out in front of her. In her hand she held a small glass with a dark red liquid in it. As she sipped it she looked through the window at the scene of events outside.

He made his way through the throng at the bar and ordered a jug of ale, puffing at the pipe as he did so. With the jug held by the handle in one hand as the other tried to clear a path through the crowd that surrounded the bar, trying not to spill the beer. Once clear of the group around the serving area he walked over to the fireplace, where he put the jug down on the wooden shelf above it.

Florence looked up at him and smiled, before turning her head away and continuing her study of what was happening on the outside of the bar.

"My name is Wiley – I have just bought two of your cows."

"I know I was watching. I am very pleased to meet you". She was again looking up at him and smiling.

"They look fine animals." He was trying to find a way to start a conversation.

"At Cormack's that is all we deal in. Why would you be buying cows - you don't look like a farmer, and if you were I would know of you?"

"I live in a cottage around the corner. I normally trade out of Liverpool buying meat for the butcher shops."

"Oh – I see." She was taking a sip of her drink. "Perhaps we could supply you direct?" Her eyes were twinkling as she looked at him.

He was chewing on his pipe as if he was thinking about it, and then he said "How?"

"We could make arrangements for you to come up to the farm to view some stock. Just say when you want to visit and I will arrange it"

They spoke for a few minutes arranging a date for him to visit Cormack. Afterwards she finished her drink. Then as she stood up saying, "All the stock I brought here has been sold, so I will be off. Nice to have met you and see you as arranged." She held out her hand - which he found embarrassing when he took hold of it and shook it. Thinking to himself it was not what women usually do. Smiling sweetly at him, she picked up her things and walked out of the premises.

**

The Cormack farm had become very extensive in an assortment of buildings. The family had grown, not only in numbers but also in stature. They had stalls from which to sell their produce in the many markets in and around Liverpool. In some instances, Patrick had either bought or rented retail outlets in prime positions. The company's horse drawn carts were all in the same livery - similar to the shops and the market stalls, all with the corporation's name in large letters. They were well known and frequently seen on the streets of the city and surrounding areas.

Patrick had become well known to the agents in the business of selling property, and would frequently be offered premises before they were put on sale to others. Maybe that was partly due to the sweeteners he was prepared to offer, if the property was right for their purposes.

When Victoria had met Patrick all those years before, she had been swept off her feet by the attention plied to her by someone whom she had admired for some time. She saw in him, and quite rightly so, an exciting young man admired by everyone and very determined to expand the family business - she had watched as he demonstrated his skills in this respect.

After the first flush and excitement of being wed, Victoria made it clear she did not want children and whilst she was happy to look after their household, she would only occasionally allow him to sleep with her. Even then she would complain of the cold in the room and not allow him to disrobe her. Despite her reluctance Robert came along. After the second child, James was born two years later, she forbade him to come near her.

In the grounds of their estate as Patrick now liked to call it, were cottages, a line of them down a badly surfaced road adjoining the farmhouse. Patrick's sister Florence had occupied one of them when she had married, and now had a child of her own -a girl called Mabel who also worked in the family business.

As the years had gone past, the family had re-invested in their property and the farm and the business had prospered and developed into a flourishing industry. To meet the requirement for storage of farm equipment and the food they were growing and producing, the family built a range of out buildings. Each day people came to buy vegetables and other goods from the Cormack's farm. The men, workers and family alike, would rise very early to take the produce to market on carts drawn by two horses.

But despite Victoria's organising of the farm house, as the family grew, the place was not to her liking. She liked space and being organised. Most of the regular farmhands came in early in the morning for their breakfast. It was not unusual at that time of day for the household to be falling over each other in their efforts to prepare for the coming day. Patrick many months before had insisted that he and his wife move into one of the cottages which the estate owned. Victoria had been hinting for many months that this little workers cottage did not suit their needs and they required a residence in which they could live comfortably and which suited their status.

It had once more been one of those mornings when nothing was going right with all the new help they had around the place. His wife, in conversation and an occasional hint, had made it clear that one of her friends was having a beautiful house designed for her - which prompted Patrick to look into the matter.

A few months earlier he had been discussing the problem with one of his colleagues, who had suggested to him an architect who was in the business of designing houses. Out of frustration of the situation he decided to look into what was involved in drawing up-plans and the construction of their own house.

Interrupting Victoria at her morning chores, he took her into the small room they were using as an office and cleared some paper work off the desk. He asked her to sit down and explain to him what she was thinking and her requirements for her new home.

She was delighted, and with some enthusiasm described to her husband her thoughts and the first was for her own quarters with a suite of rooms. She went on to add, "There will need to be staff quarters, all this coming and going is not good enough...people must be where I know they are...and of course there must be two separate places so that the men do not mix with the maids."

Chapter Nineteen

Patrick Cormack bounced out of bed at the first sound of the cockerel in the yard. The little clock ticking merrily away on the chest of drawers told him it was 5.30; he thought to himself '*the bird was dead on time again!*' There was work to be done and the large acreage of the farm would have, by this time, labourers working on it.

The property was on the outskirts of the city. It was time for the produce that was ready for market, to be packed into boxes and loaded onto carts and be on their way.

When he arrived in the kitchen his younger sister Florence was busy getting organised for the day. She looked up at him, "Are you working in the office today?"

"No. I have other things on my mind. I want to have a talk with John about deliveries and afterwards I have seen a vacant shop on a busy road. I want to look at it, for it is in the right place and could do well selling our produce. What do you have to do today?"

"There is a farmer coming, I can't remember his name. Oh yeah - Wiley - He is interested in buying some of the cattle as he supplies butchers shops. You must remember I told you I met him in the market in Huyton, we also discussed it the other day"

"Yes of course- you mean the herd in the top field. If what I have heard and it is the same man who was chatting to you in the cattle market, I'm told, they thought he was more interested in you than cows. Anyway do you think he will pay the price for them?"

"If we cannot agree on the figure then they will stay in the top field. But if he does take them it will save us from herding them to market" She said.

"Well take care and why don't you take one of the men with you?"

"Stop treating me like a child...I can look after myself."

The buyer arrived on a horse and trailer. Florence flushed with the chance of making a sale, climbed up on the seat beside him pulling her skirts up around her legs as she did so. He flicked the reins and the horse started to move. "You had better show me the way, it is a long time since I have been this way."

"If we continue down this lane it will take us to where we want to be. We do not know where your place is. Will it take long to move them?"

"That will be my problem!" He said grinning at her.

John, Florence's husband, was leaving one of the sheds and saw the pair riding away, and wondered where they were going. He could see Patrick getting ready to leave and trotted across the yard to ask where his wife was going.

"She is showing the buyer the cows in the top field." He could see his brother in law was worried. "Why, is it a problem?"

"Do you know who he is? That is Wiley, and we should not be dealing with him - and certainly not Florence on her own."

"You look concerned. She met him in the market, and he said he was looking for a herd to buy…and that's it really."

"I had better get up there – that man has a terrible reputation as a cheat and…" He did not finish the sentence but was running to the stables to saddle a horse.

Chapter Twenty

Patrick arrived at the empty shop he was thinking of renting. The brief discussion with John had left him a little concerned for his sister but he felt sure John would cope who he had last seen saddling a horse to follow Florence. Max, the agent, had already arrived and was standing in the small shop, which had a scullery type room to the rear, and what appeared to be a rickety staircase leading to the upper floor.

"Max -it is very dirty and needs a lot of work – granted it is in the right place, but I am sure we could find something a bit more appealing?"

"I had a feeling you would say something like that." He was still standing in the middle of the shop floor watching as Patrick walked around looking in more detail of what the premises offered.

"Far too small really, by the time we get a few boxes in here there won't be room to move."

"So it is a no then?"

"Yes. I think so. Now if you could persuade the people next door to sell me their property it would be a very interesting site if we combined the two."

"If you are serious I will see what I can do?" He followed Patrick as he walked outside to look at the front of the adjoining premises."I'll tell you what we have got – a nice little cottage, well farm house really - overlooking the Mersey."

"What would I want with a cottage - or is it a farm house?"

"Well I would have thought a busy man like you would want somewhere to get away from it all and relax." There was a pause while the two men looked at each other. "It is a nice place, not too small - and it has stables for the horses and room for the carriage as well. There is also a fare size piece of land to go with it"

"So what is wrong with it?"

"Nothing! And I mean nothing. There has been some tragedy in the family that own it, and they need to move on. The price is very cheap for what it is." Patrick's eyes lit up at the word cheap.

"And you think it would fit into my portfolio?"

"No doubt about it - keep it a year and you will make nice money on it."

"Alright let's go and see it."

On the journey to see the cottage, Patrick asked Max, "I think you and I get on very well?"

"Yes. But that is a funny question?"

"Not really - you are very good at what you do, and no doubt the people that employ you look after your interests. But you see I need someone who could look after my interests, and take some of the work load off me. I thought you may be that person?"

"Coming out of the blue – I would have to think about it." There was a small pause in their conversation. Finally Max said. "What would I be doing?"

"I would want you to act as my right hand man. Covering the office and answering any queries when I'm not there. I would also want you to carry on doing what you do now, looking out for any suitable properties that would fit into my portfolio. Working for me full time and any property you find will be for me to consider."

"Sounds interesting"

"We will talk about it further when we stop to eat."

Before the day was out, instead of buying a shop Patrick had bought a farm house overlooking the Mersey, and had an agreement to employ Max.

In the meantime, Florence was showing her buyer the way along the lane. On each side the fields stretched away with farmhands working the land. Some were bent double as they sowed seeds, others controlling the large shire horses as they towed the farm implements.

As they trotted along, he started to ask her about the cows and how many there were. Suddenly she felt uncomfortable as surely she had explained all this in the market, he must have remembered?

They continued their conversation, but she could not help feeling that he was more interested in looking at her instead of where they were going.

Arriving at the field she jumped down from the seat to open the wooden gate into the meadow, in doing so, her long skirt had caught on the wagon and it took a few moments to unhook it. She smiled up at him feeling very embarrassed and turned towards the gate.

The animals curious of the interruption to their feeding looked up, and the leader of the herd walked nearer to them.

Wiley got down from the seat and walked round the vehicle, ambling over to where she was standing looking at the beast. "There you are -you will not find finer cattle anywhere." She felt him brush her arm and she pulled away half turning to him as she did. She felt nervous and looked around her, but could see nothing but fields, some with men working in them.

He took her action as a signal, in a time when women did not go out on their own, he had been surprised when she had accompanied him without a companion.

He took her hand saying, "Perhaps we can talk about you first before we discuss the price for the cows." He pulled her towards him, one hand touching her breast.

Florence was struggling and trying to avoid his lips. In the distance she could hear the pounding of a horse on the hard ground. Wiley was more interested in his desire for her than to hear them, but when he did they were very close.

The mare which John had chosen came into the field with a thunder of hooves panting hard, which frightened the cows who moved further away. The rider jumped from the saddle and rushed over to where his wife was standing. He pulled her to one side and using the riding crop in his hand; he slashed the newcomer across the face and then as he turned, started hitting him across the back. Wiley was running to get on to his rig and as he did so he flicked the reins hard encouraging the horse into a trot; the wagon skidding round as it left the field.

John held his wife in his arms asking her if she was alright. She was still trembling and nodded her head. "I'm alright now - but I was very frightened."

They both returned to the farm house very shaken by the experience. Florence was arguing that as Patrick had made her and her husband responsible for running the estate, then she must have some freedom of movement. Nevertheless she accepted that it was dangerous to wander too far from the safety of the house especially with a strange man.

Chapter Twenty One

Armed with all the information his wife was expecting for a new home, Patrick made his way into the city to seek out the architect he had been referred to. It was late morning and very cold when he drew his black shining carriage to a stop outside a row of tall red brick houses. The first floor sash windows had a name in gold leaf lettering on them- 'Benjamin'. Below was the word 'Architect'.

The door was answered shortly after Patrick knocked on it. After a brief introduction between the two men, he was led into a reception room on the ground floor. On one wall was a black cast iron fireplace with a glowing coal fire, warming the room. The rest of the space was sparsely furnished with a large drawing board on its own stand occupying most of the space, with the exception of a large solid table, "So, Sir, what can I do for you?"

Death for a Starter

Benjamin was harassed, he had been in the middle of designing a timber roof structure on a large industrial building, which is no easy task and needed a lot of concentration.

"My understanding is you design houses..." Benjamin interrupted, "That is what architects do, and other things of course - Sir." He immediately had an adverse reaction to the Irish brogue, although after all the years his visitor had been in England, it had mellowed and was hardly noticeable.

Patrick was feeling uncomfortable as he did not like Benjamin's attitude. "In which case, that is what I require."

"Yes and so do many other people – what do you want a little two up and two down?" He had turned to a set of drawers where he took out a blue print, laying it on the table. "There you are, Sir. We can add an outhouse if you so wish. Where shall I send my account?"

Patrick looked down at the sheet of blue paper with the outline in white of a small terraced property. "Sir, you obviously do not realise who I am, and yet one of my shops is just down the road from here...and you have the audacity to offer me a hovel. We have rabbits living in better homes than the thing you have just put in front of me."

The other quickly gathered up the offending document and returned it to the drawer which he had left open. Realising the roof structure would have to wait while he attended to his visitor.

An hour later they were still sitting side by side at a drawing board used for the purpose of deciding on the initial design. By now they had the basis of a layout and were looking at ways to improve it.

Benjamin was speaking, "We have agreed that as one enters the front of the property they go into a large hall – now if the staircase was to rise immediately in front of them it could divide let's say here," pointing to a spot on the drawing, "And the left hand side could go to your wife's rooms in the wing of the house. Do you like that?"

"Excellent, I should have a similar suite of rooms nearby. But before we work out where they are, my wife is insisting that the servant quarters are totally separated, so that the footmen and the maids have different sleeping quarters in the house."

"How I have achieved that in the past is to have the females in the roof space of the property, the men's quarters in the basement off the kitchen and other work rooms."

"But we would not want the maids going to their rooms using the staircase off the hall…"

"No, no of course not we will put in an extra staircase so they will be able to go to their rooms without disturbing the household."

"Will it also mean they will have access to the outside, if so we will have to make sure it is secure?"

The discussions continued into the afternoon, when Patrick left he was reasonably happy with the layout of his new home. He was confident when leaving that Benjamin could work out the technical details of the new building. The architect after his new client had left, reviewed the discussion which had taken place, and had a feeling there were going to be many more meetings.

Chapter Twenty Two

Josh and Clementine were in their late teens; both had gone to university and on her grandfather's insistence trained in accountancy instead of the more female pursuits of the time. They were now both employed in the railroad business, which their father had been in since arriving in America. And of course as their grandfather owned the company, they both knew eventually that they would be joint owners.

The two houses that the family lived in and owned, overlooked Central Park and also originally some of the land surrounding them, which had been sold off for further development and had made the family very wealthy.

Owen was now in his twentieth year since arriving in New York and had not been back to his homeland. He had not heard anything other than a brief note of the death of his brother Curtis. So it was with surprise one morning when he received a letter from a firm of solicitors in Liverpool informing him of his mother's death. They also informed him that his children had been made heir to their parents' estate in the official will. Separate letters had been sent to each of them.

Josh and Clementine were ecstatic at the news and started planning their trip to England. They had been bombarding their father with questions of what they were to expect. He tried to describe his homeland which was so much different to the life style the pair were accustomed to.

Owen told his two children of the family holdings in England and Ireland describing Huyton Hall and its surroundings. He also explained that the farm he had been brought up in had been sold to another family, but that had only represented a small portion of what the family owned.

The pair were anxious to go and see what their inheritance was. After discussing the travel arrangements with the family, it was arranged for them to go by steam ship to Liverpool.

Chapter Twenty Three

In one of the terrace cottages in the small town of Huyton, Wiley was again preparing to go to the weekly cattle market which was held each Thursday morning. Next to the door that leads down a set of stairs into the cold damp cellar from the small front room of the property, was a dirty cracked mirror hanging from a nail. It was an item he had found a few years earlier discarded on one of the rubbish tips to the outside of town.

He looked into the frame at the image of himself and fingered the scar on his cheek, which was just above the full beard covering the lower part of his face. It was where John, Florence's husband had struck him with the riding crop he had been carrying when he had attacked him. A look of anger entered his eyes and the feeling of revenge consumed him. His thought on the matter was *'That he had not deserved it as he had only been trying to be friendly with the lady'*.

Outside the door of the room that lead into the street, he could hear a herd of cows being driven to the pens in the market where they would be sold to the highest bidder. He struggled into his black woollen long top coat. Opening the door, he watched the cattle ambling past, being encouraged by the herdsman and two black and white spaniels. He nodded to the man whom he recognised from other visits to the selling area and was rewarded with a wave of a hand. He was also waiting for two of his friends and looked up the street, framed on all sides by houses of different shapes and sizes, which had been built piecemeal, to the town people's requirements over many years.

Florence and John had arrived at the pens a long time before, having driven a flock of sheep which they had manoeuvred into one of the steel fenced enclosures. They had rounded up the animals earlier in the day and then had taken the long slow walk from the farm, following the creatures. It was time to retire to the Tavern for refreshments before the days sales started.

Wiley followed the cattle along the street exchanging small talk with the two friends who had arrived shortly afterwards. As the last of the cows were put into their holding area, he looked up in time to see Florence and John entering the hostelry.

Death for a Starter

This was the first time he had seen them at the market since the incident in the field. He thought to himself perhaps this was the time to have his revenge. Turning to the two men beside him he said "That woman who is going into the Tavern – she owes me - it was because of her I got this." He was pointing to the scar on his cheek.

The clip clop of horse hooves made him turn round. Coming down the road across the cobbled surface was a horse pulling one of the Cormacks four wheeled carts. Driving the vehicle and on her own was Mabel sitting on the high seat with the reigns in her hands controlling the animal. He watched as she manoeuvred the rig to the far side of the market place. It was then that he noticed she was not wearing a skirt but men's trousers.

Mabel got down from her perch and secured the horse to a pole and then climbed onto the back of the wagon. Standing up she held onto the back of the seat. A hush fell over the crowd, there was some cat calling about her not wearing a skirt. She stood there smiling, the trousers looking baggy around her waist and the legs rolled up above her footwear.

In the Tavern, Florence and John had settled down to their drink, pleased to be able to relax before the sale started. When the silence fell over the crowd, they looked at each other in surprise. John turned and looked out of the window, "What is Mabel doing here?"

His wife followed his eyes and putting her hand to her mouth muttering and repeating what her husband had said. "What is she doing?" and then more forcibly. "John - I have had enough of that girl - I do not care about any arguments. She is off to boarding school to see if they can put some sense into her, and teach her not only manners, but also where she fits in, in this life."

John shrugged his shoulders, stood up and went to the door. As he stepped outside he could hear Mabel, looking very young and a bit foolish wearing the outsize trousers standing on the trailer addressing the crowd. "Ladies – I come here today to ask for your support. The men have their clubs, it is the men who rule the country and our towns and I ask why shouldn't women do the same?"

Her father had heard enough and started to make his way through the gathering of people; some of the older men were waving their fist and shouting "We don't want any of that nonsense here." John had reached the cart; behind him Florence was standing on the steps to the Tavern, with everyone looking at Mabel.

Wiley who had been making his way towards the Inn, nudged his two friends, "Quick, don't miss this opportunity. While everyone is looking in the other direction, go and get her and take her to my cottage. Go down the alley beside the Inn and take her in the back way – I'll be there getting things ready for my guest."

John was looking up at his daughter, "Why are you dressed like that – I think you should go home and get dressed properly."

There were 'boos' and heckling from the crowd with fist waving. The herdsmen were trying to calm the animals down who had become unsettled because of the noise. Mabel was feeling very uncomfortable and trying to shout above the confusion, demanding to know why is it that only men wore trousers?

Outside the tavern, the two men grabbed Florence from behind stuffing a dirty rag into her face as they took hold of her. She was struggling and trying to kick her assailants as they quickly pulled her backwards into the alley and into the back lane, which ran behind the cottages on the main road.

At the far end of the lane was a group of children playing 'hide and seek'. A scruffily dressed small boy, the seeker, was leaning against the wall and pretending to hide his eyes, whilst counting to twenty before he could try and find the others.

Mabel was screaming at her father and pointing to the Tavern, he could not understand why - thinking she was being difficult about her dress mode.

Florence was dragged, still struggling, into Wiley's stone built cottage. He was giggling to himself as she was carried in. He pointed to a chair he had arranged in the middle of the room, with ropes and other ties he had put round it. "See this you bitch" he was pointing to the scar on his cheek. "This is all your doing." He was standing in front of her. She was tied helplessly in the chair. He slapped her around the face. "Pretending to want to sell me cattle - instead making eyes at me - wanted a little bit of fun didn't you?"

She was shaking her head and trying to spit the rag out of her mouth. The two other men stood behind her laughing.

"A nice face like yours would look better with a little mark on it, like the one your friend did to me – perhaps not so little." He was fingering a knife and stroking the blade.

Mabel was getting down off the cart, her father shouting at her to get back up and to go away and get dressed properly.

She grabbed John's hand, "Father." She screamed at him. "Two men have taken mother." She pointed to the alleyway.

"What are you talking about girl?"

She started pushing him towards the Inn "Quick! Mum has been dragged away by two men." He turned and looked back at the Tavern. "She has probably gone inside." The crowd had quietened down although there was still some whistling and shouting by a gang of youths on the far side.

Despite her insistence John still looked inside the drinking house. It was only then that he looked at his daughter saying "What happened?"

"Father, I keep telling you – they came up behind her and dragged her down the alley." She was pointing in the direction Florence had been taken.

He looked around him searching for assistance, "Help." He shouted, "My wife has been kidnapped – somebody has dragged her away down this alley."

The men nearest stopped what they were doing and came over to him, as he shouted "Follow me."

Around the square people quickly became aware of what was happening, as the news spread from mouth to mouth. The crowd going down the alleyway was getting larger. In front, John was looking around him trying to find out what had happened to his wife.

With a dirty face and knees, wearing short trousers and with a runny nose, the young lad was standing at the end of the alleyway by the start of the lane. "Mister?" Although he shouted, his small voice barely carried above the noise of the crowd that was following. John sick with worry, hardly noticed the young child who was determined to be heard and not ignored, and ran over to Florence's husband and grabbed hold of his coat.

"Mister - I have been calling you."

He was not looking at the boy he was trying to see where Florence could be. "What do you want son?"

The boy was holding out a grubby hand, "Two men carried a lady into that house over there, she was struggling and kicking." He was pointing down the lane. "For a few coppers I'll show you which one."

John was too busy looking around him and not really paying any attention to the boy. Suddenly he realised what he was saying. "Where boy? Which one?"

The urchin pointed to his outstretched hand. With a sigh John dug into the pouch at his waist and retrieved a few coins, putting them into the small, grubby hand.

The kid ran down the lane and stopped outside a gate and pointed to it.

Somebody shouted "That's Wiley's place." When John heard that, it brought further fear into his mind.

Wiley was grinning and waving the knife around, touching her cheek with it whilst his two accomplices shouted encouragement. He put a little pressure on the knife and a trickle of blood ran down her cheek.

Florence struggled harder trying to release the bonds. The two men behind the chair were laughing. Wiley said, "How do you like that bitch?" He was waving the knife in front of her nose, touching the tip with the point of the instrument.

Crash! The sound came as John, using his foot with all of his weight behind it, kicked at the door and watched as it collapsed inwards. Wiley dropped the blade and dived for the front door of the property, pulling it open and running up the street.

As he neared the top of the High Street he heard his pursuers shouting behind him. He turned quickly into one of the small alley-ways between the buildings and with total knowledge of the area, he managed to lose his followers. Knowing that if he returned to his home then he would be quickly found, he made his way to Liverpool, where he knew that at his brothers daughter's house, he would be able to hide. Deep in the knowledge he would not be able to return to Huyton.

Back at Wiley's house, John was busy releasing his wife. Mabel, who had followed her father, was wiping the blood off her mothers' cheek. Florence said, "Thank the Lord you were in time, it is only a graze but a few minutes more, who knows what he would have done."

Wiley's accomplices had tried to follow him through the front door of the house, but in the crush of the two of them trying to get through the small space, they got apprehended.

Both were dragged backwards down the street and thrown in the primitive jail opposite the market. After a week living in the cramp condition of the prison, they were paraded in front of a magistrate to hear their punishment. The following day they were taken to the common where a large post had been installed many years previously – the post had one use- the chastisement of criminals.

The towns' people gathered around and there was a carnival atmosphere. Tinkers set up stalls to sell their wares. Clowns were entertaining the crowd with their juggling and other tricks. A gap opened up through the throng as the two men were forced to hobble through them, their arms chained to each ankle.

One was held in front of the crowd so he could see what was going to happen. The other was tied to the post with his arms around it. With one quick movement a broad tall man who was holding a long handled whip, stripped the prisoner's shirt from his back. There was a cheer from the crowd. To one side, the man administering the punishment was dressed totally in black. His next prisoner watched his colleague being chastised, in horror. Knowing he was next, as he watched the whip being raised and thirty lashes landing on his friends back. Each one was being counted out by the cheering crowd, who clapped and shouted when they saw the first blood from the wounds appear.

Two weeks later they were at the dockside, still in chains, being pushed and dragged along as they hobbled in the restraints fixed around their legs. Again there was a crowd who had gathered to watch, all cheering when they were enforced on to a ship to be deported to the New World.

**

It was getting dark when Wiley finally made it to the front door of Ida's home. Pushing it open he found her by the fire-range knitting. "What are you doing here?" was her greeting as she stood up to see who had entered.

"That is a fine way to greet your uncle? I thought I would come and stay here for a while"

"Alright - what have you been up to and who is looking for you?"

"No - one" he said hastily. "I'm just bored living in that small town, and I thought I would see if there was more excitement in the city."

"And may I ask who is going to keep you? Because I ain't - I am starting a new job tomorrow and I will be living in - so you will have to look after yourself." Although she knew she was only going for an interview - but she felt confident she would be accepted.

"That's alright Ida – you do what you have to do. It will be alright if I stay I can look after myself?"

"Suit yourself, the rent will be due at the end of the week – I'll leave you to pay it."

Chapter Twenty Four

The following day Florence was adamant about Mabel's future. After a brief discussion with her daughter, arrangements were made for her to go to a school in Liverpool where she would live in. The school was well known and respected where the off springs of the gentry were sent to become ladies. Also to be taught on the finer points of running a house.

It was a Friday, and Patrick had got into the habit of visiting his favourite coffee house in the afternoon before the weekend. As was usual he arrived outside the premises' and the stable lad took charge of his horse and carriage. He also knew that the head of police sometimes visited on the last day of the week. He was not disappointed when he saw him talking to a group of men in a corner by one of the curtained windows.

The group moved aside to let him join them, shaking his hand as they did.

"Hello Patrick." The policeman turned and waved to one of the serving girls to bring over another beer. "How is business?"

"Just fine - I was hoping you would be here, I was wondering if you knew of a man named Wiley?"

One of the others in the group said, "He's not the sort to get mixed up with."

The policeman looked at the speaker, "Why...who is he and what has he done?"

"He buys cattle and sells them to the butchers – but I'm told he is not past stealing them." said one of the group.

The law man looked at Patrick "Has he been stealing your stock?"

"No - what he has done is far worse than that! Some time ago he forced himself on to my sister Florence. But he did not get his way with her, her husband John, beat him. This was in one of the fields at the top of our place, he came with the pretence of buying cattle. Just recently he kidnapped her, and again John was just in time to save her, although not quite in time as he had used a knife to cut her cheek. Wiley had tied her to a chair. This happened in Huyton, last week." He was angry with the thought aand was speaking quickly

"I'll send someone round to interview your sister and then we will try to find this person. Have you got an address for him?"

"His address is where he had held Florence. He fled from there when John found her. Surprisingly he has not been back!"

"Have you any idea where he could be?"

"No. I want to put a reward up for information leading to his arrest."

The newspaper man in the group asked, "How much for Patrick?"

Patrick thought for a moment, "Would ten pounds be about right?"

The policeman laughed. "For that money I will go and look for him myself, what do you say fellows – we all go out and have a look around this day?" The group laughed, knowing he was not serious.

The reporter said "That is great - that will make nice headlines in tomorrow's newssheet."

The policeman was as good as his word and a few days later a detective arrived at the farm to interview Florence.

Chapter Twenty Five

Around this time was when the first portable petrol and diesel engines to work machinery were being developed. First it had been with steam power and other fuels, but the new combustible fuels were smaller, lighter and easier to handle.

In 1885, news of a French firm started to filter through who were trying to develop a horseless carriage, using a petrol engine to drive the vehicle. Most young men were fascinated by this rumour, but in general very few believed it, dismissing it out of hand as impossibility. The memory of the steam driven cars that had been developed and their problems were foremost in their minds.

But when in the same year the French firm had a very basic machine built and running. (*In reality it was to become the fore runner of design for years to come, with an engine in the front driving the rear wheels, a passenger area in the middle, and a boot to the rear*). Only then did the people with the most diehard objections believe it.

Robert had been well educated in a private school paid for by his parents. His brothers and sisters had also followed him to have a higher education than most. One evening the family were sitting in the living room around a roaring log fire, and as normal after the evening meal, the men were discussing events about business and other news in general. The ladies had retired to their own room.

Death for a Starter

James, who was a few years younger than Robert was speaking. He was sitting in a chair around the long dining table and leaning his arms on it. In one hand he held a glass full of beer. The froth was spilling down the side on to the table, whilst in the other he held a pipe, the white smoke drifting out of its bowl, a habit he had started the previous year. "Father, I know we have discussed this before, but what is your opinion of the horseless carriage, do you think they will ever be able to improve on them? Quite frankly I do not believe this story about the French – anyway what do they know?"

Patrick, although sitting at the table, was half turned away from it putting another log on the fire where he had been warming his hands. It was where he normally sat in the evening. Like his second son he was also smoking a pipe, which he removed from his mouth as he turned to look at James.

"I have mixed feelings about it. We have seen the spread of the railways across the country all driven by coal fired boilers to create the steam to drive them - also steam ships have been in production for a long time. In fact your grandparents came to England in one in the late fifties. But when you apply the same technical knowledge to a car, the system is too bulky to make it work."

He stopped and appeared to be thinking as he looked around the table at each one of the men. "As you know when we bought one – which by the way, is laying in the shed going rusty and worth nothing – at the time we were very excited thinking it was going to be simple. No more horses to feed or to harness a sometimes reluctant animal and to put up with their occasional strange ways. We all know what happened to get the carriage moving- we had to spend a lot of time to get the fire hot enough to create the steam, and then we were limited to the distance one could travel by the length of time the fuel would last and how much we could carry."

He paused again while he inhaled smoke from his pipe. "No -the engine that made it move was too bulky, and any way when it did go it was difficult to stop. I think I'll stay with the horse and my carriage."

Robert, his blond hair out of control drooping over his forehead, was looking down, busy undoing laces and taking his brown leather boots off. Listening to his father with a smile on his face, this quickly turned into a grin, when he looked up as he pushed his hair back into place.

"Father we know all that, but it is in the past. Things are changing. I am convinced of what we read about the French is true. Without a doubt someone will find a way of either developing a new engine that will drive a new type of horseless carriage or perhaps making the steam version more efficient."

"Yes, I agree with you son, but how long will it take, I don't know,- and does anyone? In the mean time we carry on with what we have."

James was responsible for travelling around the companies premises ensuring things were as they should be and ensuring that the employers were working efficiently. He was not going to be put off.

"I like my horse and I like her funny ways and I cannot envisage going to one of the shops and stopping outside in something billowing smoke and choking everyone. I think things should stay as they are. Anyway those noisy things have got no mouths. Where would one put the sugar?" There was a little giggle around the table.

Robert was kicking his boots into the nearest corner of the room. "James you have no vision, things will change and then you will be the first to show off your new machine."

"No! While you are driving around puffing smoke and fumes everywhere I will be going along with my favourite animal that will still be pulling my rig."

Robert joined in the conversation again. "You are too old fashioned – Father. I'm the engineer and I look after and repair the machines on the farm. I would like to try to make a horseless carriage. There is an old farm machine, in fact it is next to the old boiler driven car you were talking about – I would like to see if I could do something with that. I could also pull the other thing apart and use some of its mechanics"

"Are you that determined? Leave it for now and we will look at the cost and other requirements later. Anyway where would you obtain an engine? You are not proposing to build one of those as well? No - forget it for now".

"Father I know of someone who is designing such an engine. I will go and see him because we will need to know how much such a piece of machinery will cost."

"As you wish son – but do not spend too much time on it."

Chapter Twenty Six

Mabel had spent her young life growing up in a family who worked together, sharing the tasks that needed doing either around the house or in the farm and fields. Now instead of the comparative freedom of being at home, she was in the strict system of the boarding school. She found it difficult to understand why women should be taught to do household chores, whilst the men had a far more interesting life and upbringing.

When she followed the other children and went to a school where she lived in, something she had refused previously, she was determined to change the other girls in the same year, to her way of thinking. Mabel would stand at one end of the dormitory preaching her thoughts about equality for women, and even after the bell was being rung in the corridors, for lights out, she would continue with her talk until one of the staff intervened.

Death for a Starter

Her best friend was Roxy – who said it was her stage name and hinted that "It is really Rose." She had red hair in comparison to her companions' mousy brown. They were seen everywhere together and Mabel learned that her colleague came from a family of circus acts. Her parents had felt that she needed an education for a few years before travelling further with them.

Since a child she had learned the art of knife throwing, and would frequently go into the grounds of the school to practise her art. Thomas the grounds man, whom Mabel had a crush on, would help the two girls to build a frame so Roxy could practise her skill. She would draw a chalk line on the frame representing a person, and then throw the knives to just miss the outline. Sometimes she would invite one of her class mates to stand inside the chalk line, while she practised throwing - although she was very good nobody would take her up on her proposal. Then one day, one of the pupils did take her up on her offer. The group of people watching cheered, and the girl stood in front of the board whilst pretending not to be scared.

Roxy's six throwing knives were held in a scabbard on her shoulders at her back and to throw one, she would reach over and with a flip of the wrist the tool would skim through the air to its target. The first hit the board by the target's leg – the second in quick succession was a little higher. Then the third pinned her arm to the board, by going through the sleeve on her blouse.

After this episode the school banned the use of knives in any form of practice. Roxy was devastated, and without her practising sessions she got very bored with class work. One afternoon she told Mabel that she was leaving. With a shocked look on her face was her friend's only response. And then, still staring she said, "But what will you do and where will you go?"

"I'll find work somewhere - I do not know where, as yet. And then I will try and find my parents and join the circus - far more fun than staying here."

With a cry and a hug they both agreed to keep in touch, and the next morning Mabel saw her friend walking out of the gate.

Mabel tried to settle, and now her friend had left there was no excuse to see the gardener and she started to pine for him. After having been at the school for nearly a year which was part of a four year programme, she was expelled for disruptive behaviour. Her mother, Florence, was not very pleased as she had wanted her daughter to be a lady and marry into the gentry. So consequently, when she arrived home finally from school, a heavy discussion took place and she was told, "Another place at a different school would be found for you"

"But mother I do not want to be taught how to crochet or to work as a seamstress. Why can't I do what men do?"

"Because you are a woman and I want you to be a lady not a farm hand! Now listen to me I do not want you growing up with this nonsense in your head. Tomorrow you and I will go back to the school and you will apologise for the upset you have caused. We will see if they will re-instate you. Now do you understand?"

"Mother! I am not going back to that school or any other. I am going to stay here and help in the family business, because I think that is where I belong."

At that moment Mabel's uncle Patrick came into the room, "Hello Mabel. What are you doing home?"

"She has been expelled for preaching women's rights."

Patrick smiled, "Well done you."

"Patrick I do not see what is funny. She is going right back there tomorrow and she is going to apologise for the upset she has caused." This was said with some force.

"Mother, I just told you, I do not want to go back and I am not going back – I want to work here with the rest of the family. What do you think uncle?"

Florence said "So Patrick you tell me what I should do – her education is important…"

Mabel interrupted with a sigh. "I have already told you I do not want to learn about embroidery - I want to do something more productive. Please Uncle Patrick help me, why can't I be taught about writing and figures – surely that is more useful to the family than me making dresses which mother wouldn't wear? Anyway she buys hers in the fashion house"

"I think, Florence we should think about what the girl wants, and see if we cannot come up with an answer that would suit everybody." Patrick looked at his niece, smiling he said. "You are starting to look a bit chubby, you'll soon lose that with a bit of work in the fields!"

Tears welled up in her eyes and she was shaking her head. "I don't think so uncle - I am with child" She started to sob. Pulling a handkerchief out of a pocket, she started dabbing at her eyes.

Her mother was shocked, and the two adults looked at each other horrified, with Florence saying, "What are you telling us?"

"You heard me mother." The girl murmured.

"Does the school know about this?" She was talking very sharply and her face had gone white. Patrick just stood there, looking on in horror as his smile faded away.

"I do not think so. But they knew what we were doing because they caught us doing it."

Patrick found his voice "Is that why the school expelled you?" Mabel nodded her head.

"Who is this man?" Florence felt like screaming and she was having difficulty in controlling her voice.

Tears were flooding down her face as she answered "Thomas...he's an odd job man at the school."

"Odd job...what are you saying...odd job man – in a girls school" She had turned away with her fist clenched. "Are you telling me they have an 'Odd job man' wandering around?"

"He has a workshop in the grounds. But we hardly see him."

"It seems to me you did more than hardly see him." Her mother was shouting.

Patrick intervened, "I think we should go in the living room and sit down and go through this quietly." He was opening the door, "Come on Mabel this way."

For a moment Florence did not move and then she angrily marched into the other room. She sat on the arm of a chair, and stared at her daughter.

Patrick was trying to calm the situation. He also wanted to take control as he did not think his sister was in a frame of mind to deal with the problem. "This Thomas what is his other name - did he force himself on you?"

She was shaking her head feeling very shameful, but part of her wanted to protect the lad. "No...it was nothing like that. His name is Thomas Fisher."

Her mother interrupted, "Are you telling us you let him do it and you encouraged him." Mabel was looking down as she nodded her head, whilst her mother was putting her hands up to her face.

Patrick spoke "How long have you known him and how old is he?"

"I met him about six months ago and we have been seeing each other when-ever possible – the school does not allow it so it was not easy…oh and he is a few years older than me."

"So what does this young man say about him being a father?"

"He does not know. And now I don't know where he is and I want him. We love each other."

Patrick stood up "It is not too late for me to go to the school to see if I can find this Thomas Fisher - the school must know where he lives." He walked to the door and left the room.

"So young lady, how did all this come about?"

"Some time ago you visited me in the sick bay…? Do you remember the door would not shut properly? It was a few days after your visit and I was getting better. Suddenly Thomas arrived and was fiddling with the door; he did not know I was there. By then we had known each other for some time. I was lying on the bed - he looked up and saw me. I was

petrified and embarrassed as I only had my night things on."
She turned away wiping a tear from her cheek.

"So he came over and took advantage of you - anyway
where was the nurse?" Florence said.

"I don't know. I think it was time for the midday meal
so she was probably in the dining room. We were chatting and
I remember he finished the work on the door. He closed it and
came over and sat on the bed." She looked at her mother and
shrugged her shoulders.

"Was that the only time?"

Mabel shook her head. "No. Seeing him was never
easy. We knew if we were found together he would lose his
job. Then yesterday I had a free break - I should have gone to
the library to study. But I had not seen Thomas for some time,
so I went in search of him. He was in his workshop and I
wanted to tell him about the baby, and ask him what we
should do. But he took me in his arms...one of the teachers
must have seen me - she was probably looking out of one of
the windows in the school, when I went into the workshop.
Thomas was being very passionate and was doing things with
my clothing - I didn't mind as he had done it before. Then
there was a shout from the door and the teacher was screaming
and after that things happened very quickly."

Patrick had taken his favourite carriage to go to the
school. The school was in a state of shock st what had
happened in the past few days, and he found it difficult to gain

access. Finally after some persuasion he managed to have a meeting with the head, who was devastated when she heard the news of Mabel's condition. Patrick explained he was going to insist on a marriage, and would she release the address of where this Thomas fisher lived. Not wanting any scandal and realising he meant no harm to the man, she opened a desk drawer, took out a folder which she flicked through, and then wrote down the details and passed them to him.

It was a dirty narrow street in Liverpool, the cobble stones laid in the wet road were troublesome to the hooves of the horse drawing the vehicle. Each building had an overhang on the top floor some with women hanging out shouting to their neighbour. Scruffy children were badly dressed and as in many parts of the city, were holding dirty hands out for some reward.

The carriage was a tight fit in the road, its shining black exterior a strong comparison to the dirty grey/black of the buildings. The top of the coach barely missing the second floor overhang of the run down houses.

Like many of the other hovels in the road, the address he wanted was as bad as most and in need of repair, with dirty windows and torn curtains visible through the stained glass. He used his stick to knock on the wooden door, with the paint of many previous years slowly peeling off.

A short pause and a voice shouted from above, "Who is it?"

"My understanding is that Thomas Fisher lives here – is that correct?" Patrick had moved back into the road to see who was speaking.

"What's it to you?" She was hoping for some reward.

"I would like to speak to him, please. Is he in?"

Sensing she was not going to get anything from her caller she answered, "He's downstairs in his room, with his man friend. He'll come out to you."

There was a squealing noise as the door of the property opened. "Yeah - what do you want?"

Patrick looked at the tall slim young man; his unkempt hair falling over his shoulders and showing the first signs of beard stubble. He was adjusting his dress and fastening the belt on his breaches. "My name is Cormack – that should mean something to you - as you have had your way with Mabel my niece."

"I don't know what you are talking about – I don't know any Mabel."

"Yes I think you do. You were the odd job man at her school and you have been meeting her for at least six months. Now get your things because you are coming with me."

"I'm not going anywhere with you - and you can't make me." A small crowd had gathered in the street, and someone shouted "Go on Thomas! You tell him."

"Alright!" Patrick took a deep breath. "Let's do this the nice way and I'll tell you why - if you don't come with me, and make an honest woman of her, you my lad are in deep trouble. I will see to it that you will not find any more work. That will be just for a start. Anyway you are going to find it hard because you have not got a reference" He saw the others' face change. "I think you are starting to understand me?"

In the reflection of the glass in the dirty window, he saw someone creeping up behind him. He swiftly turned, raising his stick. The youth who had been moving stealthily up behind him quickly turned back.

He returned his attention to Thomas. "I think you had better get into the carriage. We are leaving"

"I'll just go and tell Wiley that I have to go."

Patricks face changed into a grin, he was thinking to himself, *'Can it be the same Wiley? Surely there are not two of them'* Saying out loud, "Is that the same Wiley who used to live in Huyton?

"Yeah! I used to go to him for a bit of fun - but since he's moved back he comes round to me."

"Oh!" Patrick was shocked but also delighted. "Don't worry I need to speak to him - I'll will tell him that you are coming with me."

He took hold of the boys arm and led him to the carriage. There was some shouting from the on lookers and someone said, "Where you taking him mister?" None of them were acknowledged. He guided Thomas onto the vehicle, took the horse whip out of its holder and turned to the door of the house.

He pushed open the inner door. He stood there in the doorway in shock, which passed very quickly. The room was scruffy with clothes littered across the floor. Wiley was leaning on a couch, his clothing in disarray.

Patrick smiled. "We meet at last." He flicked the whip, and after many years of using it to control horses, he could crack the leather above their heads without hitting them. The end cracked in front of Wiley's nose. He quickly pulled away from it with fear in his eyes.

"I'm very pleased to find you here. I am going to do you a favour." The lash crossed the room again cracking in front of his face. "I am going to save you from a public whipping at the post on the common, instead it is going to be a private one, and of course afterwards you will not be deported – at the same time I am going to save myself ten pounds." His face had widened into a grin, but his eyes were not smiling. "You are going to understand after tonight, not to go anywhere near my family ever again."

Wiley, full of fear was crouching, looking around him as the whip again cracked near him. He was trying to work out a way of escape. There was not one as his accuser stood in his way.

Death for a Starter

There was a whistle as the lash came back with more force, hitting him around the hips. He cried out. Wiley turned as the next onslaught came screaming to him, and wrapped itself around his back, the end bringing a sharp pain in his side.

At ten strokes, with his opponent crawling along the floor screaming, Patrick stopped. "I think you understand me, next time you are dead." He pulled the pistol he always carried from its holster and held it to his opponent's head, then deliberately fired a round into the floor, to create further fear. Wiley screamed again and crawled away from his aggressor, blood seeping through the dirty white of his shirt, his trousers around his ankles.

Patrick turned to the door, "Get up you coward – get yourself dressed. Mark my words, leave my family alone - it would be better for you if you were to leave and go to live elsewhere." He slammed the door behind him.

Out in the street the crowd moved away from him as he put the whip back into its holder and climbed up into the vehicle. Taking the brake off and flipping the reins he started to move along the street with the crowd following behind

"So you like playing with men?" He did not wait for an answer. "What took place today we will keep to ourselves? But if in future I catch you – or hear of what you have been up to, you will get the same as I just gave him. I do hope you understand me." He pointed his hand in the way they had come. Thomas was nodding, "Where are you taking me?"

Death for a Starter

"First of all you are going to have a bath and then we will find you some suitable clothes." He turned to look at him and with a flick of the reigns, "You are going to go down on one knee and propose to my niece. "After which I am going to give you work. And then you are going to make an honest woman of my niece - some time very shortly. Before that you will become a truthful, sincere and upright man that the family can be proud of."

Arriving back at the farm the couple sat on the couch holding each other's hands. Florence was relieved she was not going to have to face a daughter having a baby without a husband. Patrick was also pleased with the result. His niece would have a husband and by the look of it a loving one. He would also gain - what he hoped would be a loyal worker.

Thomas Fisher, could not believe his luck. With his friend Wiley's screams still echoing in his head, he knew Patrick was not the one to cross.

Chapter Twenty Seven

The Guttenberg family had originally arrived in England from their native Germany, where they had been involved with another group in the manufacture of machinery. For some time there had been a difference of opinion between the two groups - whether to progress into developing the latest technology of steam power or continue with their main production of farm equipment. Agreement could not be reached which resulted in a break up.

With the capital they had brought with them they set up a small works to look into the development of small engines driven by steam. They also decided that their name was a little clumsy for the English language and changed it to Bergen.

It was in the fifth year of settling in their new country that Cecil was born and very much to their delight, when at a very early age he became interested in what the family were producing, and started to study the ins and the outs of anything mechanical.

Cecil, now in his late teens had been involved with steam engines from the time when he could first start to walk. This had been at his father's engineering workshop. There was very little he did not know about mechanics, and he was employed by the family firm developing and making improvements in steam engines, to drive ships and trains. He had also done some work on the same power plant to drive a horseless carriage.

But the young man felt it would be possible to use other fuels, so that the power source in the machine would be a lot smaller than the bulk of a steam system. This would also mean doing away with the need to burn coal or other bulky fuels to make the engine work.

Cecil set to work with the help of a grant from his wealthy father, who was as equally keen on his sons' idea, and offered his support. After searching for a few months he rented a workshop which would suit his needs, and started planning his design for an engine which would run on liquid fuel.

Although he had made a study of engineering and had total knowledge of how a steam engine worked. He knew a petrol engine would be very different.

An engine running on steam had a piston which was pushed down when the water vapour entered under pressure.

He was aware that petrol exploded when in vapour form, so he understood he needed to be able to inject the fuel into the top of the piston. The difference between a steam engine and a petrol one was that you had to ignite the vapour to make it explode and drive the piston down in order to turn a crank. But that was the problem - how to make it explode?

In his well equipped workshop he set about making an engine which would run without the use of a coal fired boiler and steam. Progress was slow and although he understood the basics of why it should work the reality was very different.

On one occasion with a design in place, he allowed the fuel to enter the cylinder where he had designed a system to ignite it. He retired to a safe place before the ignition took place. There was an explosion and a flash of flame and a very loud bang. Pieces of steel hurtled around the workshop and his work lay in scraps, scattered around.

He was a determined young man, and after reading other peoples progress or non progress, he continued on his quest to develop an engine which would work. After months of trial and error, making parts and assembling them on a bench, he was convinced he had come to the end of his efforts as he was certain the new design would work.

Again taking care to be in a secure place, he started his new petrol driven engine. It roared into life, blue smoke pouring from the exhaust. He looked in wonderment at his achievement and was looking forward to spreading the news especially to his father. A few minutes had past, and it was still chugging on the bench when he noticed it was changing colour. It was going red, and then with a groaning noise it stopped and the sump of the little motor split. He now knew he would have to find a way of dissipating the heat it was creating, and to find a way of cooling it while it was running.

Chapter Twenty Eight

It was a bright summer's day when the ship from New York city docked in Liverpool, and Josh and Clementine were leaning on the rail of the great liner, fascinated at all the activity going on around the vessel as it was slowly moored alongside the quay. The arrangement was for them to go to the shipping company's hotel, where they were to be met by the solicitor dealing with the will and their inheritance.

The smartly dressed legal man, who was in his sixties with thinning grey hair, greeted them warmly. After they had had refreshments, he ordered a Hansom cab to take them to his ground floor office with golden wood panelling and polished flooring, a short distance from the hotel.

Sitting around a table in his office, he explained that he had looked after the affairs of the family for a long time. He took over the work when the elderly founder of the law practice had retired. In front of him he laid out the relevant papers concerning the transfer of the estate into their names. He then arranged for the three of them to go out to the property the following day, so that he could show them around and introduce them to the staff.

It had been forty eight hours since leaving the ship when the carriage arrived, to take the pair and the solicitor to Huyton Hall. When they arrived they were both surprised at the size of the property. They had thought their homes in New York were grand, but this old sprawling building took them by surprise and was going to get some getting used to.

After introductions to the staff, the butler suggested that he should show them around the large house, and afterwards the head gardener would take them around the grounds, "If there was time to do that today." They accepted his offer and along with their new friend the legal man, they set off.

The three of them with the butler started in the vast hall, followed by the rest of the owners' living area. Finally a little exhausted after climbing stairs and walking down the various hallways, they went down to the kitchens and the other work rooms on the lower floor of the grand old house. The solicitor had retired to the drawing room some time before, enjoying a pot of tea.

The butler said "Now that you have seen over the house, perhaps you would like to see the gardens. I will get the head gardener to show you around."

Clementine looked at him with a smile on her beautiful face. "Not quite all, I think – we have not been through that door." She was pointing to a door in a corner of the laundry room.

"Yes madam – you are right but it only leads down to the cellars and is very little used these days."

"But I think I would like to see them – what do you say Josh?"

"We have come this far and I do not see why we should leave that part out." His American accent was more pronounced than his sisters.

"I have left it out, Sir, because it is dark down there and not very clean – cob webs…"

"Never mind, you seem reluctant for us to see it. So let's go." Josh started to walk to the door. The butler retrieving a key from a set hanging from a board and lighting a candle opened the door, and the three of them went down the steps into the vaulted roofed cellar.

Clementine thought to herself, after they had walked round, '*Nothing but old equipment and things which would have been better if they had been thrown away instead filling this place up with useless items. But she did wonder what was in the chest, gathering cob webs in the corner, and thought it would be exciting to open it.*'

Chapter Twenty Nine

"Patrick – I told you yesterday that I wanted your help today, in interviewing the applicants for the staff of our new home."

He looked up from the desk where he had been studying the latest drawing the Architect had sent to him."And I told you Victoria that there was plenty of time" he said in a resigned voice.

"And I made it clear to you, I want to start some maids now so we can train them in our ways then they will be ready when we open the new house." Victoria was being very firm with an aggressive attitude.

"Alright – alright, I'll be there in a minute when I have finished what I am doing. Where are you interviewing them?"

"Outside in the yard - we can see them better there."

It was some time later that Patrick walked out through the rear door of the house. Standing in a line was a row of six young women all dressed in a similar style with long black skirts and white tops worn tight around the neck. His wife was near to the end of the line talking to one of the girls and studying a piece of paper which she held in her hand.

Patrick walked over to the group, and strolled down the line introducing himself. Each girl bobbed their knee and gave him their name. He arrived at the end of the line as Victoria his wife moved away. He had a strange feeling as he was looking at the last applicant as she then in turn bobbed her knee saying, "My name is Ida, Sir." He had a strong urge of wanting to touch and hold her, and felt excited at the thought.

He could not remember feeling like this before. He wondered *'Why this girl? None of the others make me feel this way.'* She lifted her head the high cheek bones on her face turned into a beautiful smile. He looked into her deep blue eyes which were locked into his. His hands started to tremble, he forced himself to turn away, and he walked over to his wife. He was fascinated in her and could not stop himself from turning round to look at her again, standing erect and proud. His eyes looked over her slim body and her uplifting breasts, for the first time in his life he experienced a strong desire of wanting a woman.

"What are you thinking. They all look acceptable to me and anyway the agency would not have sent them if they were not satisfactory." He said to his wife.

"Yes I was thinking the same." She turned to face the group. "We will go into your duties later. In the meantime we have two cottages reserved for your accommodation. That is where we would want you to live until the house is built and finished, then you will move into the top floor. If you will please follow Margaret she will show you to your quarters"

As the group moved away Patrick was finding it difficult to take his eyes off Ida. Watching her, her hips swaying in the long black skirt, as she followed the remainder of the group. His heart did a flip as she turned and smiled at him.

He spun round hoping his wife had not noticed, but she was too busy talking to one of the other staff.

Chapter Thirty

On the odd occasion while making their way to the city markets, one of the rare horseless carriages of the time would chug past them. Robert, who was now in his twenties, would look on and dream. He was fascinated by the new engines driving these machines and he heard and read stories of others putting them into different types of vehicles.

One morning he did not want to delay any longer, with the space the family had and the knowledge he had gleaned from books and his teachings at university, why shouldn't he build one?

He approached the small engineering works in the City of Liverpool where he met Cecil, who was developing a small twin cylinder petrol engine and with a little help from his new found friend, Robert started to build a horseless carriage.

Death for a Starter

The result was an odd looking four wheel vehicle which he had spent months constructing, working late into the evening in one of the outhouses on the property. He did not receive any help from the family which he constantly had to placate, always trying to enthuse them with his endeavours. He especially gained his Fathers' displeasure, who was convinced the whole effort was a waste of time and money.

The great day came and with the small two cylinder petrol engine purchased from the Liverpool engineers, he started the machine into a chugging rattling vibrating motion, all balanced on four wooden wheels with steel rims taken from a cart.

During the building phase there had been a problem of how to connect the drive chain to the rear and also a brake. He settled for the drive to be on one side and the braking mechanism on the other, which in reality was a wooden pad he could pull on to the outer rim by a lever next to the driving seat. The other problem was how to have a system that would steer the front wheels and at the same time put brakes on them, so he settled for just one rear wheel to do the braking.

The three dogs were barking at this noisy contraption now parked outside the shed where it had been built. The engine was running and the family were standing around. The ladies were in long flared dresses. His brothers stood in long coats with waistcoats tightly buttoned and slim breaches, most had soft felt hats on their heads. The rest of the staff were also there to celebrate this great day. His Father, Patrick, stood behind them on the doorstep of the house frowning. He had moved there from the front of the group, when to his discomfort, Ida had stood next to him, giving him fluttering feelings.

Beside the family, the staff had been invited to join the group, which led to their family and friends arriving to witness this exciting happening of a carriage moving without a horse, people had been looking forward to the event for many months. Two year old Helen was with her mother who had closed the village shop to be here, the child was standing at her feet her little hands were clapping copying some of the others. Robert was a little sad, as he could not find his younger brother Sean, who would miss this inaugural occasion.

**

Sean had left earlier that day and had walked into the town of Huyton. He had heard from his friends that there was gambling in an upstairs room in the Tavern, and they had told him it was very easy to win a lot of money. And that is what he intended doing today.

As he entered the room, one of the owners Tom nudged his partner, John, who was standing next to him, they were the sole owners of the establishment, saying "That is one of the Cormacks."

"I'll go and see what he wants." He was most surprised when he discovered that Sean wished to gamble, and even more surprised when he revealed he did not know how to play, as he had never seen a pack of cards before. After sitting down at the table with green baize over it, he was taught the wonders of pontoon, where you have to make the value of a set of cards in your hand up to twenty one.

Sean had brought a few coppers with him and one of the men showed him how to bet and they started playing the game. Very quickly he was winning and the coppers piled up beside him, he was grinning all over his face, and kept playing with the coins in front of him. But then he lost one hand, and continued to lose after that, as the dealer's cards were always better than his.

The time came when he ran out of money. Not only the small amount of cash he had brought with him but also what he had won. He went to get up from the table but the croupier encouraged him to stay saying, "Don't worry you will soon win the money back again."

But he didn't, as the expert dealing the cards made sure he was not going to win, although he let him be the victor in a few hands just to keep Sean sitting and continuing to play. The amount he owed the house increased. The two owners were very happy while they waited watching the young Cormack getting deeper in debt. They were certain they would be able to recover the money from his father.

After a while, the two men came up and stood behind his chair. By this time Sean was feeling very tearful. John the taller of the men put his hands on Sean's shoulders; Sean winced as he did so. "So young man, how are you going to repay us for the fun you have had this afternoon?"

"I don't know – perhaps if I continue playing I could win it back?"

The two men laughed. "No, no son we don't think so. Would your Dad help? He's Patrick Cormack isn't he?" As he spoke, he softly smiled.

"He doesn't know that I have come here." Suddenly the thought flashed through his mind that he had been cheated and he had walked into a trap.

"Well - so as to keep you out of the Debtors Prison we had better go and find him"

Sean started to sob, "I don't know where he is." He stood up and faced the two men, his hands were trembling. "I don't think so; it has got nothing to do with him."

They grabbed him by the arms. "Never mind! We will start at your house or shall we go straight to the prison?" They half dragged a struggling Sean out, and into a pony and trap.

**

Waving to his onlookers, Robert climbed into the make-do seat, which on this trial model was nothing more than a piece of smooth, six inch wide plank of wood secured to the frame of the vehicle. He had not bothered to put a back rest to it - that could come later.

With no gear box, to make the thing move all he had to do was pull a lever on his left hand side so that the primitive clutch would engage the rear wheel via a chain drive, which had come off their old steam driven horseless carriage. The tiller, in between the two levers, would steer the front wheels, and the first of Roberts creations would be off. At his calculation, its speed would be about two miles per hour. He knew that was slow, but he was not worried, as he knew that in the future he would be able to improve the machinery and make it go faster.

Sitting on the primitive seat, he turned and waved again to his family and friends who had come to watch this momentous happening. Taking a deep breath and although not a deeply religious man, he said a little prayer and crossed himself.

The clutch lever was on his left hand on his right, a similar lever that would release the rear brake. First he had to advance the throttle, which was a little lever fixed to the frame of the very basic vehicle. At first he could not find it, as his coat had fallen across it. He gave it a little turn and to his delight he heard the engine increase not only its noise, but also it was going faster, and blue smoke was pouring from the rear. He was about to pull the clutch lever towards him, and at the same time getting ready to push the brake lever away from him.

There was shouting at the gate. Looking round, he could see two men with Sean sitting between them. Robert secured the machine and waited to see what was going on.

John the taller of the two was speaking, "Patrick Cormack, we have your son here and he owes us a lot of money - what are you going to do about it - as he says he can't pay us?"

Sean's father walked over to the gate. "And how much would that be?" He had a soft smile on his face which the men should have recognised as a danger signal. Sean was shouting, "Don't pay them father - they cheated me."

The two men in the trap told him to shut up, and answered with an exorbitant amount. Sean spoke up again, "It wasn't anything like that much."

Tom answered, "But we have the cost of our time and expense of having to come here to collect, what is owed."

Patrick was leaning on the gate and was looking at them giving the impression he thought it was funny, and then he said "Very well. Wait there."

With that he turned and went into the house. The two men Tom and John still sitting in the trap smiled at each other. It did not take long before they heard footsteps behind the trap they were sitting in. They turned to see Patrick pointing a shot gun at them. "Now very slowly get down and keep your hands where I can see them. There is also someone else watching you from the other side, so be very careful." Patrick was still smiling.

They looked around and saw James had come into the yard, from the back of the house. He was also pointing another shotgun in their direction. They both got down, one each side of the vehicle.

"No son, you stay where you are...don't get down. Now one of you will have the boy's money, so give it to him."

They passed some coins up to Sean. Patrick was not taking his eyes off them, all the time a small smile on his lips. "Now I want you to stand together. And then my other son James will make sure you have not got anything on you that might hurt someone."

Two pistols were taken off them. "Put the pistols into the trap son. Sean - you drive it back to where it came from and James will follow and pick you up. You two - I hope your shoes are comfortable because you are going to walk back."

Tom said "I can't do that I've got a gammy foot."

"Then it is going to be hard for you."

The pony and trap was in the process of being turned around as James went off to get transport for the small chore he had been given. Patrick looked at the two men. "Please do not try and take liberties with my family again, because next time I will make you really sorry - not just a walk back to town. Do you understand me?" Although fuming inwardly, they both nodded their heads.

Although a little worried about the two wanting revenge, the family congratulated their father on the handling of the situation. They turned their attention to the horseless carriage awaiting its first trial run. Before that could happen there a delay while they waited for the return of the two boys. On their arrival, Robert restarted the engine and climbed back onto the seat. He waved and then turned his attention to driving the machine for the first time. He pulled the clutch lever towards him, and at the same time releasing the brake, by pushing the identical lever to the clutch, away from him.

Robert had misjudged how fast his horseless carriage would go, and had expected there would be a smooth genteel forward motion. Instead the machine lurched forward. He was sliding backwards off the seat so he grabbed hold of the tiller to try and steer it and still managed to hold on before completely leaving the contraption. If he had fallen he would have landed on the ground behind his pride and joy.

Struggling back to try and gain some control of the vehicle which was now hurtling across the yard, not straight as he wanted, Robert found that the one driving wheel was sending it in a curve and hence it was heading for the far fence. He needed to stop it. With a struggle and a lot of effort, he could hear his family clapping in the back ground. Robert managed to get control by regaining the makeshift seat. Using his right hand he leaned forward and reached out for the brake lever and pulled it hard. The wooden block vibrating above the steel rim of the back wheel moved onto it with some force. The wheel locked and skidded on the gravel surface. The carriage spun round, in the opposite direction it had been travelling, and slowly turned over on to its side.

Helen had thought it was all great fun and had been running after the prototype as fast as her little legs would carry her. Robert who had nothing firm to hold on to was falling to the ground, landing heavily on one arm, he felt it crack as the

192

bone broke. At the same time the machine was lying on its side one wheel was left spinning in the air. Petrol started to leak out of the makeshift fuel tank which fascinated the young child and she was reaching for it as it reflected in the rays from the sun.

Family and friends came rushing over. The ladies were holding the front of their full skirts up out of the way of their feet as they sped across the ground. They and the men were all intent on helping Robert up on to his feet. But he could smell petrol and while they were still fussing around him, he was imploring them to get out of the way as he could see the child reaching for the liquid.

Slowly they moved away from the stricken vehicle and were so intent on asking him if he was alright whilst brushing the dirt from his clothing. They were not looking at Helen who was laughing and thinking it was very exciting.

Despite the severe pain in his arm he turned to look at his work. As he did so, a small flame had ignited from the leakage, and was quickly gathering momentum. The child stepped back but not quick enough. The edge of her long dress caught alight. Robert pushed his way past the gathering and grabbed hold of her - as the fire engulfed what was his pride and joy. The flames were starting to spread up the child's dress, whose laughter quickly turned to a scream. He put Helen on the ground and rapidly removing his coat wrapped it around her smothering the flames. It was then he realised he had picked her up in his damaged arm. The child was sobbing, but the heat from the fire, which had damaged her clothing, had had no effect on her skin.

Robert with his arm in a sling, carried on with the work of making a vehicle that did not need a horse to pull it. In the past few months he had learned a lot in the building of his horseless carriage, and now had an idea of how to make another machine. This one would be far better and a safer machine than his first attempt. But Patrick was not so keen saying "Enough is enough, we nearly lost the baby. I want an end to this nonsense, and let us carry on with what we are good at."

**

Two very tired men arrived back at the Tavern; one of them was limping as a large blister had developed on his heel because of his badly fitting shoe.

"God I hate that man" Tom, the smaller of the two said.

"What do you intend doing about it?"

"I don't know." He removed his coat and lowered himself into a chair. Bending over he started to remove his boots. "What I do know is, he's not a man to mess with."

The other man was standing near the bar getting a drink. "I know someone who would happily take him down a peg or two."

The one sitting looked up at him. "What is the name of the person who is on your mind - I bet I am thinking of the same chap?"

"Well I reckon it has got to be Wiley? Because if that is the same person you are thinking of - that man has a very special hate for the Cormack family."

"Yeah but he has left Huyton. Do you know where he has gone?"

"Probably back to Liverpool. He has friends and relations there. We could make a few enquiries to see if we can find him. Somebody must know where he is."

Chapter Thirty One

Patrick walked across to the stables where he selected his favourite grey and led her to his shiny black carriage feeding her a lump of sugar as he did so. He was backing the animal into the shafts of the vehicle when his son Sean came over to help him.

"Where are you going Father?"

"Well, Sean my son, sometimes a man needs to get away and after the fiasco I have seen this afternoon…horseless carriage baa! I am going to my club in the city." The club was really a coffee house.

Sean smiled up at his Father, "Can I come with you - please"?"

"Of course, but when you are a little older and then I'll let you drive the Phaeton, I think you will enjoy that."

Death for a Starter

"Oh Father, please let me come with you?"

"That is enough - I said another time, but not now...anyway you should be helping Robert to clear up the mess he has made. Also you have caused enough trouble for one day" Sean walked away in a sulk.

Patrick drove out of the farm gate and along the rutted road heading for the city. As he did so he passed the Atlas Club, which he looked at with envy. He had applied a few years before to become a member, knowing that it was where generation after generation of the city's elite in the business world met and had been doing so for nearly one hundred years. But membership was restricted to the few and the very wealthy. He was determined that one day they would beg him to join. In the mean time he would do what all the other business men did, who could not make the grade to join the very up market club, which was to go to a crowded coffee house, where the latest gossip and news could be gleaned.

He drove his carriage over the cobbled surface of the city's roads weaving in and out of the afternoon traffic. He steered the grey around the various carts and carriages which were going about their business in this part of the city. He was looking at the people shouting and jostling on the side of the road, where market stalls were set up. There was a certain joy in listening to the buskers selling their wares. He looked on with interest when he passed the stall where an employee was selling the family's produce, and was pleased to see a queue of people waiting to purchase from the display of fruit and vegetables.

Death for a Starter

The coffee house he frequently visited was one of the more up market ones with imposing premises just off the main thoroughfare. As he turned the mare into the small road, he saw as usual the valet standing outside who he knew would look after his rig for a small fee, while he enjoyed the pleasures of the premises, although he rarely ever did. There were gambling tables in the rear and upstairs other activities were waiting, where young females knew how to keep a man, especially a wealthy one, happy for a few hours.

In one of the corners he managed to find a seat in the noisy crowded room with a steady murmur of laughter, chattering and the occasional raised voices, whilst at one end a minstrel sitting on a chair played a fiddle. The atmosphere was heavy and filled with smoke. He was about to sit down when there was a little bit of excitement as one of the gamblers from the rear was dragged across the room and thrown out into the street for cheating at the tables, landing in the stinking wet gutter.

Patrick had collected one of the newspapers on entering the premises, and with a special house beer on the table beside him, he sat down to read the latest news the paper offered. He was sitting with a group of others at one of the small round enamel topped tables. A female started to sing. Looking up, he glanced at her as she sang in tune with the fiddle. He found it a little embarrassing as her skirt was not full length and only just reached below her knee.

Ignoring the others who were sitting with him, he was busy turning the pages of the broadsheet looking at things that interested him. He felt a thrill of excitement when he saw a large advertisement in one of the pages of the Liverpool Mercury for the water flush toilet which had been developed a lot earlier in 1851 - the first of which was shown at the Crystal Palace Exhibition in London. As he read through it his excitement was growing.

On the far side of the smoke filled room, Patrick could see Benjamin his Architect who he was in discussion with, to design a large house to accommodate the Cormack's growing family. He thought of it as more of a palace, which he intended to call Tullamore, which in Irish means big or great. It was the name of the small village about fifty miles west of Dublin from where he had originated. He had left there with his parents when he was a young child, but even then as a youngster he had spent his days toiling in the small holding.

Benjamin was a small round tubby man with a prominent beer belly. He was in his late thirties sporting a small goatee beard, which at that moment he was stroking with his left hand, whilst holding a glass of ale in the other, and his small silver pince-nez reading glasses balanced on the end of his nose as he studied a news sheet laying on the table, not noticing that some of the beer had spilled on to his waist coat. He looked up to see Patrick standing next to him, and he thought to himself *'oh no not another change to the plans,'* which in the past, to his annoyance, had been frequently made.

"Benjamin, have you seen this?" He was pointing to the advert with a raised voice against the noise in the tavern. "I think we should incorporate these into the design. I also think we should have one in each bedroom…well not quite in the bedroom itself but in a closet, or the dressing rooms."

The Architect put his glass down and stood up, "Yes I have seen them before." He was slightly annoyed with himself because he had not offered the facility to his client. So he went on the offensive. "Do you realise what the cost would be? You don't just put one of these pan things on the floor – we need to include a drainage system, Sir. And that has to go somewhere, after all it is not like a chamber pot you empty in the morning…Anyway I did not realise you had that sort of money for this house of yours?" As soon as he said it he knew it was the wrong thing to say to his client especially in front of other people. Patrick had gone red in the face.

People were starting to listen to the conversation. "Sir, I am not too certain if that is not an insult…but this time I will let it go. But Sir, you have a way of putting things in a way that I find offensive, and as for emptying things in the morning that is why I want this new fangled thing included in the design." By now the crowd were laughing. Someone shouted '*go on Patrick you tell him.*' Patrick picked up his cane where he had propped it at the table, touching the top of his top hat making sure it was secure.

Feeling embarrassment at the humour others were showing, he turned saying, "We will meet in your office tomorrow morning to decide where…these things will be situated." He said sharply pointing to the news paper, "And Sir, I am surprised at you, that…and I am sure you must have been aware of such a facility…you did not include them in your original work. Good day to you Sir. I will see you in the morning shall we say at 10.00 o'clock sharp?"

Benjamin replied, "Yes Mr Cormack I will be waiting for you." But he was thinking to himself that he did not like the man and was wondering if he could pass him off to one of his colleagues, but then again the work was an interesting assignment and worth a great deal of income.

The next morning Benjamin realising he had upset his client was up early to make the changes he had been requested to make, and as the hour of ten approached he was nervous wondering what Patrick would say - realising he had made him look stupid also suggesting he could not afford the house in front of patrons in the coffee house.

Exactly on time he saw, what was becoming a familiar site of the shining black carriage pull up outside his property, after waiting for a coal cart to move out of its way.

Patrick marched into the room and saw the drawings on the large flat table, Benjamin was trying to please when he said "I have made the changes you requested yesterday – and I think they fit in well."

His visitor did not comment but leant over the work and using his finger he was tracing where the design had been changed. Picking up a pencil he crossed a part of it saying, "That will not be good enough – there needs to be more space I'll be sitting on the thing while I am trying to get dressed."

"Patrick." He was trying to be polite. "I started at six this morning to work out the changes you requested and I think they will work. That part you are pointing to will give an area of five feet by five feet, in my view plenty of room."

"I tell you sir it is not big enough." Patrick had put the pencil down with some force breaking the point. "Why is it you do not listen to what I tell you – I think you are out of your depth, the project is too grand for you."

"Sir, that is an insult...." Patrick interrupted.

"A lot less than the insult you shouted at me yesterday in front of all my friends and others."

"For which I apologise. It was something said on the spur of the moment"

"Nevertheless it was very embarrassing. I have put some thought to it over night and have decided that we are parting company. I will pay you for your work up to date and very shortly I will give you instructions of where to deliver the drawings so they can be completed." Benjamin was shocked he watched as his client recovered his hat and coat and left without another word.

Chapter Thirty Two

Robert had set to work after his disaster of trying to build a horseless carriage. Every day he retired to the workshop where he had purchased and installed drawing equipment. Another six months were to pass and after many a sleepless night sitting at his drawing board, he had designed what he knew in his heart was the machine that would make them millions.

During that period, he had spent days and sometimes weeks, with the owner Cecil, and the friendly staff at the engineering company in Liverpool, discussing his requirements. The result was a lightweight two stroke engine which would fit snugly into the frame of his new design.

Robert had seen other people's attempts at a two wheeled vehicle. He had also read reports of some of the disasters that had happened in people's endeavours to manufacture a motorcycle which was reliable and safe. He was determined not to make the same mistakes. His Father was not being very helpful and was worried about the cost.

But as the project progressed, he started to admire his son's efforts and tried to give him some form of encouragement.

There was no stopping Patrick's eldest son, and another year was to pass and with a great deal of help from his engineering friends, he pushed his new two wheeled machine out of the workshop.

By now the family, which had first arrived from Ireland all those years before, through their hard work and determination had built up a substantial business. The small holding had expanded in size by the purchase of neighbouring farmsteads of arable land adjacent to the original plot which now covered an area of over one hundred acres. Throughout Liverpool and the surrounding towns, either in the markets where they had permanent pitches to sell their wares, or in the various shopping centres and High streets, there were Cormack's outlets with their shops being smart and fashionable.

Robert was also well known in the various coffee houses and night clubs he visited, where his peers went to relax and enjoy themselves, which included business people and also news men who met to exchange stories. During the period of the construction of his new machine, he was frequently asked how progress was, and with some leg pulling, as everyone wanted to see the finished result.

On this particular day, which turned out to be warm, bright and sunny, the new machine was going to be displayed for the first time, although there was a dark rain cloud hanging over the far side of their estate. Far too far away to be of any concern, a large crowd had gathered to view the wonderful device. Robert knew firsthand the local media of the time, and had invited them to view his new creation.

One of the reporters in the crowd standing in the yard at the rear of the house, called out, "What are you going to call your machine Robert?"

Robert had only thought of it as a machine, a motorcycle. It did not have a name. He suddenly thought and the name came into his head and he said "Dauntless."

There was a short clapping of hands and the reporters were busy writing in their note books.

There was nothing but accolades for his invention. The story was repeated in the National newspapers praising the motorcycle and its features. Dauntless was then described in detail in the Auto press, with the result that people across the nation wanted further details and some started ordering the machine.

Robert went cap in hand to his father to help in the funding of production. Patrick was impressed and swallowed his pride and promised all the help he could give, asking what was needed to build the machines where people had given firm orders.

His son smiled at him saying "Father what I need is a larger workshop than the one I have now!"

Chapter Thirty Three

Benjamin was not a happy man. He was mad with himself for losing a client. He had been busy at his drawing board, when through the window he saw Patrick's carriage pull up outside and park in the road. He watched once more as the local children, most of them dressed in rags, ran around the vehicle holding out their small grubby fists for hand-outs. He thought to himself *'I suppose he has come to pick up his work and settle the account.'*

Putting down his pencils and other drawing equipment, he had been using on the adjoining table, he took off the smock he wore when working, and substituted it for a jacket. When he heard the footsteps on the stairs, he opened the door to his studio to receive his guest.

"Good afternoon, Mr Cormack. How are you on this fine day, your work is all ready for you?"

"Thank you, Sir, I am fine. I have come to talk to you about some additions to the property. I have decided to continue with your good self, because we are too far in with the design to change at this late stage. But that is not to say that I have completely forgiven you"

Benjamin thought to himself, '*oh no not more changes*' but instead he said, "And what would the changes, be Sir?" He was thinking to himself, *How am I going to find the time to do the work*' as he was so busy with other clients.

"I have just come from my club...well coffee house – same thing really. There has been a very large explosion on the other side of the city, and the word is it was caused by gas leaking. So I want all the lighting in the house changed from gas to electricity. You can manage that?"

"That is not a problem I have already incorporated that in the design." Whilst thinking to himself '*That is a relief.*'

"Fine - there is more. Can you please lay the drawing out showing the plan of the property?"

The Architect opened a long narrow drawer, part of a set standing to one side. He pulled out the flat sheet of blue print, laying it on the table where both men could lean over it.

Taking a silver propelling pencil out of his inside jacket pocket, Patrick started pointing to the outline of the outhouses that were shown on the plan. "I want to move this block, what I need is to bring the stables forward to here." He pointed to an area on the blue print. "And where we had decided the stables were." He drew a line around the area. "I want a workshop built. I want this workshop to be about one thousand square feet in size, and have facilities like water closets and electric lights, similar to the house."

"Excuse me Sir. But none of that is possible."

Patrick looked up puzzled "May I ask, why not?"

"Because, when you told me you did not want me to continue I have taken on other clients which need my attention-----"

** **

Eventually the rift between the two could not survive their working relationship. A short time later, Patrick instructed another practise of architects, Clayton and Partners, to draw up the plans for the new workshop. They were given further instructions for changes to the house, and then it was discovered that other modifications were needed, as some of the original drawings were defective in that the measurements did not tally.

It was some time later that work finally started. The original house was pulled down in phases so as part of it could still be lived in, whilst the construction and remodelling of the property got underway.

The new property was to be built with local grey stone, so popular and readily available in the north of England.

The new house, with fourteen bedrooms, was built with stables and other out buildings, to garage the growing number of vehicles needed by the homestead and the business. There was also the workshop where the motorcycles were to be built.

The layout of the house was designed in a traditional style, with the kitchens in the lower part of the property where the footmen and the male staff lived. The maids' accommodation was in the top floor of the house which was part of the roof space, with a stairway leading to it on one side of the building.

In the owners' accommodation, besides the bedrooms and other living quarters, there was a large room for dancing and holding gatherings. It was finally completed after a few years of construction. The new building took up the original size of house and the rear yard the Cormack's had purchased when they first arrived from Ireland fifty years before.

Prior to the completion of the house, Robert had been very busy producing the motorcycles. Patrick recognised that the machines could make money, so he allowed the workshop to be completed before their home, much to Victoria's disgust. Robert had run many advertisements in the trade press, so with all the advertising and the accolades about the machine, not only by word of mouth but also in the trade press, orders flowed in and very quickly he needed help.

The small engineering works he had been dealing with were in difficulty. They were not covering their costs of the various engines they were designing for other people. With the help of his father, Robert made Cecil an offer to buy them out and in return to employ him and his engineer, to concentrate on the engines for his machines.

This served two purposes for Robert and the manufacturing process; he had twice the space for production, and he was employing engineers who knew and understood the mechanics of the vehicles they were building.

Chapter Thirty Four

Since the loss of two babies at birth, Victoria, Patrick's wife had refused to sleep with him. In the old house she had moved him into one of the spare rooms whilst she kept the original master bedroom. In the new property she had a suite of rooms with her own bathroom in one wing, and he had something similar in a different part of the home.

Victoria had been brought up in a house with strict Victorian values. She could see no wrong in having her own quarters and not sleeping with her husband. As she saw it, her duties to him had ended when she had produced his children, and now it was time to get on and enjoy her own pleasures.

The third child Margaret, as a toddler, used to help in the farming by doing simple jobs supervised by her mother. As she grew older she was taught the skills of knitting and crochet. Finally going to an all girls finishing school where she was educated in the wonders of being the lady in charge of her own home.

It was at finishing school, whilst mixing with the other pupils that debates would take place in the dormitory of the unfairness of only men being able to vote and why should the man be the dominant sex? These discussions had a lasting effect on her, although she felt there was little she could do about it as most women were prepared to accept what had always been.

Margaret had very strong views about the difference between the sexes. She found it a pleasure discussing this with her cousin Mabel, who was more determined than her and was passionate to change the system. But her cousin, strangely, found a certain amount of pleasure in needlework.

On leaving school she helped in the family business. One day when she was in her teens, her father brought home the architect Clayton, who was to redesign their new home. With him he brought his son Walter, who was in his first year training to join his Fathers practice. When he asked her to go to the opera with him, she accepted with a flutter in her heart and her Father's approval.

Margaret had been courting for some time, while the new home was under construction. She made it known that her intention was to be married to her by now, long-time boyfriend, Walter He was now in his third year of training to be an architect at Liverpool University.

As the house neared completion, plans were being made for a grand opening of the property. There was to be a party which the elite of Liverpool would remember for years.

Much to Patrick and Victoria's displeasure, Robert had no plans to settle down with a wife. With the motorcycles being produced under the care of a management team, Robert spent a lot of time travelling to trade fairs, or following up leads from people or companies who had shown an interest in the machine.

On one of Patrick's regular trips into the city, he noticed an empty showroom which was for sale. Stopping the carriage outside what was a remarkable building, near the centre of the city, he entered and a little while later walked out with a contract to purchase the property. Robert was overwhelmed; the display area available would show his machines off to their very best.

But the fly in the ointment as far as Robert was concerned was his father, who wanted the rooms on the first floor. Including the largest and best one, of which overlooked the street, for his office. As Patrick said, "He went into the city on most days, and worked from one of the many coffee houses, so an office in the heart of Liverpool would be ideal. Also he would be able to have one of those new devices - a telephone installed." Eventually Robert extracted a promise from him that he would not interfere with what his son's staffs were doing on the ground floor, selling motorcycles

Death for a Starter

On the first morning of using the new facility it had seemed very quiet and he found he had time on his hands, so Patrick walked from his new headquarters to his favourite coffee house. The scene inside was as rowdy as ever but it suited his mood. He found a table in the corner and ordered his favourite tipple and settled down to read the news sheet.

Chapter Thirty Five

The great day for the opening of the house had arrived. Robert had other ideas for the day, and had gone into the city to call at a tavern that he regularly used. Although it was early, he had made arrangements a few days beforehand, and Molly was waiting for him. He was holding his top hat in his hand as he entered the bar, his dress coat buttoned at the front, with a white shirt and bow tie, which caused quite a stir to the early customers.

As she stood up to greet him, he looked her up and down saying, "You look nice but I think we had better find a ladies fashion shop, because mother will have a fit if she sees you in a skirt that short. We had better find you something which reaches to the floor, and a bit higher in the neck line"

"Oh Robert, I thought I looked fine, and anyway I do not like long things – I like showing off my legs." She lifted her dress a little higher doing a twirl, "You see they are nice legs."

"They are lovely - but today they will not be on show...or maybe later -but that has to be very private. We do not want to kill mother with a heart attack – do we?"

He helped her into his carriage, which shone like a star in the scruffy street and the normal kids in rags were there, holding their hands out. Driving into the shopping area they stopped outside of a suitable shop and an hour later Molly came out looking entirely different. Not quite the highest of fashion, as he had shuddered at the price, but last year's style suited her.

He looked at her adjusting her hat a little and said, "Right let's go and party."

"Robert -do I really have to wear this corset...? I can't breathe and it is difficult to move in."

"Don't worry you will be able to take it off later!"

Tullamore House was decked out with flowers and bunting. Beside its gravel drive, there were plants and trees to the verges all lit with concealed lighting, showing off the grandeur of the front of the property. Servants had been hired to help make things run smoothly, so when the guests arrived in their carriages, there would be a groom waiting to lead the vehicle away. The visitors once they had alighted from their various vehicles would be escorted into the house through its grand porch and double doors.

Death for a Starter

The couples walked arm in arm. The ladies were in fashionable skirts with their tiny waists held in with a corset, finished off with a square cut neckline blouse and puffed sleeves. All of the ladies had hair piled high on their heads, most balancing a small hat to set it off, all in the fashion of the time. Around their necks and arms were sparkling jewels. Most of the men wore long formal tail coats with white shirts and black ties, the occasional man sporting a white one.

To one side of the large property was a ballroom, where Patrick and his wife stood side by side in the entrance to greet their guests. To one end of the dance floor, with fresh flowers in vases surrounding the area of the stage on which stood a quartet playing soft music with fairy lights glittering round them.

Mabel was dressed in her finery; a long full gown in a beige colour with gold thread weaved into it. She was astonished to see the mob of red hair in the crowd of her old school friend who was serving drinks. Roxy was walking around and mingling with the guests holding a tray full of glasses with sparkling liquid, "Roxy what are you doing here? I would have thought by now you would have rejoined your Mum and Dad."

"No- I am having fun getting to know people – I work for an agency in Liverpool and they find all types of different work for me..." They were interrupted by a couple wanting drinks off the tray. She continued, "Sometimes I get to use my act with the knives."

"Good for you."

"To be honest I never thought that you lived in a place like this, and married too! I could not help noticing the lovely ring you were flashing around holding the glass. And do I spy a bump growing"

"Yes – it is due in another five months. You will never guess who the father is?"

"You mean I know him?"

"He's over there." She pointed to the nearby doorway. "He looks a lot different now – but it is Thomas the odd job man from the school."

"Wow – how did you achieve that?"

"Well after you left we got caught in an embarrassing situation and I was expelled – Uncle Patrick was having none of that – he went and found him and we were married three weeks later. I have a little cottage on the estate - you must come and visit. It is the first cottage down the side road to the left of the house."

"Excuse me are you serving drinks – or are you here to chat? I want you serving in the dining room." It was the senior agency worker.

"I had better go – oh and by the way I am working at the Tavern in Huyton as from next week. Bye for now."

After the buffet dinner, that had been served in the dining room, the guests returned to the dance hall. Victoria was pleased to see Robert had a pretty girl on his arm as they swept on to the floor in a waltz but was puzzled about who she could be. Patrick looked at his wife, indicating the couple and said, "Who is he dancing with?"

"I do not know, it is the first time I have seen her. They did not attend the opening so that she could be formally introduced...neither the buffet. Since he has moved into one of the cottages on the estate, and remember I was against it, who knows who he is mixing with."

Patrick smiled and nodded his head it was a subject he did not want to get into again.

The evening was going well and people were sitting around chatting, that is those who were not dancing - with everyone in a happy mood. Patrick thought it was time to make the announcement that his daughter Margaret was to marry Walter at St Anthony's Catholic Church in Scotland Road the following March. There was clapping all round and a few shouts from the men of congratulations.

As Patrick left the stage he was approached by Benjamin, who he had seen earlier and was surprised that he had attended.

"Hello Patrick, a grand evening, and thank you for the invitation. Clayton has done a fine job but of course it was based on my original design. I wonder if we may talk somewhere in private?"

His host was puzzled. After the bad words and arguments over the original design of the house, he did not think he would see him again. "Certainly - It is very nice of you to come. Are you on your own?" Out of the corner of his eye he could see Robert and his lady friend leaving the hall by one of the French style doors, which would lead them onto the terrace overlooking the garden. He led his ex-architect into the small room near to the front door of the house.

"Yes, I do not have any attachments – wife or lady friend."

"I did not know that. What can I do for you?" Patrick was shocked by the admission.

"It is more what I can do for you. In the past you have made approaches to the Atlas Society. What you do not know, is that I am on the committee, actually chairman of the membership committee. Your name has come up once or twice, so when your kind offer came for tonight's entertainment…….." He paused stroking his small beard as was his habit. "…I came along because I think it is the ideal time to convey to you, an offer by the club. They would like you to come for an interview with the view of becoming a member. If you are in agreement could you come to the club next Wednesday at 2.00 p.m?"

Death for a Starter

Patrick thought, '*You only really came to have a look at the house which you partly designed.*' He was wary, feeling there was something more; he went on to say, "I would be most privileged to attend. Would you please thank the committee for me?" He was too dumb-founded to say anything else, he had looked forward to this moment for years and the very man, he thought he would not speak to again, turns out to be the very person who had the influence to make it happen.

They exchanged further pleasantries as Benjamin stood up and took his leave of the party and bid his host good night.

Patrick turned to find his wife walking towards him and he could see she was not very happy. "What are you going to do with your son? I want to know – he has taken that hussy out into the garden – that woman with clothes that do not match and a hair style that is a mess…what will happen? I will be the talk of Liverpool…people will be pointing and staring I will not be able to show my face – what are you going to do about it?"

He took hold of her hand and led her into the room he had just left. "Victoria - he is a grown mature man, and a very successful business man at that. If people want to talk I do not see what harm it can do. And anyway I also do not see it is any of our business, but I will have a word with him when he returns."

"What do you mean you cannot do anything about it? Bah...he wanders into the party with some strange girl, does not introduce her to his parents, and then to upset me he takes her out on to the terrace – in front of everyone and where from there, God only knows. And you say you cannot do anything about it. There he is ruining my reputation and you...bah I am going to my room." And off she pranced. She lifted the front of her heavy skirt to go up the wide sweeping staircase, but stopped, she turned and staring her husband in the eye, she said: "Another thing - I am fed up with you ogling that maid Ida. If she wasn't so good at her work she would have been gone by now." She turned and made her way up the stairs. Patrick returned to the party, shaken by his wife's words, not having realised his thoughts and sly looks at Ida were so obvious.

When Robert had arrived at the venue a lot earlier, he decided he was not brave enough to walk through the front entrance with his partner. His mother would have had a shock at the way Molly spoke. So he had crept in another entrance and waited until everyone was at the buffet before entering the ballroom.

After leaving the dance floor, the pair had sat on the terrace. He could not help feeling how lovely she looked in the floodlights. He had intended to go back inside but he had other thoughts, and could not wait to walk her to his cottage for a night of entertainment. He was well aware that he would have upset his mother, but the thrill of bringing a prostitute home and parading her around excited him. He thought it was very funny and could not wait to tell his friends at his club. In the mean time the thrill of exploring a long full skirt and its many petticoats below and undoing that tight corset would occupy him well into the night.

Chapter Thirty Six

The day before Patrick was to become a member of the business club he had set his heart on all those years ago, he was in his office above the motorcycle showroom, with the word 'Dauntless' in an italic dark blue lettering on the fascia. He heard the door to the street slam shut and footsteps on the stairs and then the door to his secretary's room closing. There was a gentle tap on his door. His secretary Clara came in. "Benjamin is here to see Patrick." When she had first started working for him she addressed him as 'Sir' – but he would have none of that and insisted on her using his Christian name. She ushered the visitor into the front office.

"Good day to you Sir, what can I do for you? I thought our meeting was not until tomorrow."

"Good day to you as well Patrick. May I come in?"

"Of course - come in and take a chair." He led the way to where two comfortable chairs were situated beside the unlit fireplace.

"Sir, I apologise for my intrusion but I come here on a very delicate matter, which I am finding difficult to explain."

"You have me puzzled Benjamin. You don't mind me calling you Benjamin, do you?"

"That's what all my friends call me. And I think I would enjoy it if we were friends and put our differences behind us."

Patrick was smiling as he often was when he knew somebody was going to be difficult. It was a way of making them feel uncomfortable. "Of course I totally agree. So what is this delicate matter?"

His visitor was finding it very hot in the room. It had south facing windows and the sun was shining through, making the room very hot. He wiped his face with a pristine handkerchief that he had removed from his breast pocket. "Please do not take offence as none is intended - but some members feel that there may be a conflict of interest because of your Irish descent." He paused noting that Patricks' face had not changed and gave no indication of what he was thinking. "The problem is that for the past thirty years some people in Ireland have been demanding independence from England. And it has only been a few years since 1879 when the Land Wars erupted and the tenant farmers refused to pay rent…and one of the committee members lost his son in that tragic event."

"I do not see what any of that is to do with me or my family. Please go on."

"If I may just continue – even as we speak there is a revolutionary fever in your ancestor's home land. What I have come to ask on behalf of the members, if you are to join our exclusive society." He paused wiping his forehead with the handkerchief, which he had been fiddling with while he was speaking. "Would you consider using a more English name than the one you use of Cormack?"

Patrick stood up, slim and tall the opposite of build to his visitor; he started to laugh and leaned against the mantle above the fireplace. "My God man- you took a long time to ask me that. Perhaps what your committee do not realise is that I was very young when my parents came to this country. All my family were born here and none of us have been to Ireland. I certainly have not been back since my parents brought me here. Anyway the name of our main business is Dauntless, where we do not use the name of Cormack which is our name - and once a very proud name in Ireland. I would have thought by now everybody knew of it as it is on the front of our shops. Perhaps your members should ask their wives where they do their shopping and they will find out we employ a lot of English people. We are very much an English company."

"Yes we understand that, but don't you see the problem?"

With a smile on his face which was getting broader, and anyone who knew him well would know that was when he was getting angry, he said "Quite frankly no. We have built two thriving businesses here using the name Cormack. There is not a High Street in the Liverpool area that does not have a Cormack shop in it. If the members of your society will not have me with the name I have then Sir, I think that will be their loss." He turned and was looking out of the window. "I will arrive tomorrow wearing my best Cormack suit of clothing, and if someone blackballs me then so be it."

Benjamin stood up and they shook hands as they made their way to the door exchanging small talk, but his visitor did not look too happy.

The following day Patrick appeared before the committee where he was made welcome. The question of his name did not arise and after a brief interview where a few questions were put to him, he retired to a different room, so that the members could take a secret vote whether to accept him or not.

Each member had one white ball and one black. The committee secretary passed a box, with an opening in its top so each member could put his hand into it without others being able to see what coloured ball he deposited in the tray at the base of the unit. Once the box had visited each person, the chairman slid the tray out in front of the members present to show that it contained only white balls. If there had been one black amongst them, then Patrick would have been shown the door.

On his return to the committee room, he had taken the Societies oath with his right hand on the bible. There had been a lot of hand shaking and back slapping, after which he was shown around the lush premises.

Chapter Thirty Seven

A few days after the house warming party the orders were flooding in for the Dauntless Motorcycles. After many interviews with the Chief Constable, Robert managed to get an order from him for one machine, for a trial period. Everybody was ecstatic because it generated more newspaper headlines explaining it was the first police force to have a mechanised vehicle.

Patrick had settled into a routine visiting the Atlas club about once every few weeks, not finding it as inspiring as the coffee houses where he had many friends. Some of them he had got to know when he had first started visiting in his teens. At the business man's club on a few occasions the members would invite him for an evening's entertainment at the White Swan, a public house with a reputation, which he always declined. It was not until sometime later when he learned that 'Paid Ladies' as they put it, were also invited to liven up the evening.

On one occasion, he was in his favourite seat when he noticed one of the members come into the club and have a short conversation with the receptionist, and then walk out again. He did not think much of it, until he remarked to the person he was having a conversation with. "He must have forgotten something ," nodding to the door where the person was just leaving.

Patrick's companion looked at him to see if he was joking. Deciding he wasn't he said, "I don't think so – he has a lady friend."

"Oh...so why does he come in here and go out again?"

"You don't really understand?" Thinking to himself you must be very naïve. Taking a deep breath he said "I thought everyone knew. He is a committee member, he has just told the clerk that if anyone needs him he is in a meeting and cannot be disturbed."

"Oh. But he didn't go upstairs." Patrick was looking puzzled.

"Of course not he has gone to see his lady friend...mistress... who lives a few streets away."

Patrick was embarrassed and was finding it difficult to understand. He had been celibate for as long as he could remember. It had not bothered him and the teaching of his Catholic religion had taught him that the sex act was only performed for the creation of children. And yet in this place that did not seem to matter.

**

As the industry in the use of mechanical vehicles expanded, other similar machines were being developed and sold, taking some business away from the Dauntless. To help offset the competition the motorcycle was being constantly improved. But there was an urgent need, as Robert explained to his father, for larger premises to keep up with the demand.

On the outskirts of Liverpool a large steel mill which had got into financial trouble was closing down, and the factory was for sale. After a brief inspection, Patrick and his son came to an agreement with the owners and came to terms for the purchase of it. It took a few months to organise the workforce, also moving the production from the two plants they were operating to just the one. The two original buildings they kept, using the original one for storage, and where they had produced the engines as a service centre for their products.

Chapter Thirty Eight

Margaret and Walters' wedding was the following March, the reception following the church service was being enjoyed by everyone. This included most of the towns' dignitaries who had also been invited. Patrick was enjoying the many compliments that he was receiving. He had participated in many separate toasts to the happy couple from well meaning friends and business associates, some of whom had laced his drinks with stronger spirit. The bride's father was beginning to feel unwell, as he normally drank very little alcohol. Soon he was fast asleep, having collapsed into a chair.

The following morning Patrick felt a little low knowing that his daughter had now left home and was about to honeymoon in Ireland. In some ways he was wishing in all the years he had been in England, that he had found the time to visit his homeland.

He would normally go to his office in his own carriage, but this morning he felt like he needed company. Roberts cottage was a few minutes' walk away down the lane running beside the house. He was enjoying the fresh early air listening to the birds singing in the trees and hedgerows, as he approached his sons' home.

He was thinking to himself it had been a long time since he had visited him and suspected he would be surprised. He opened the rear door and entered into a small kitchen where he noticed there had been many changes since he had last been there.

Robert's Alsatian dog, who knew him well, was lying on his bed by the stove. It wagged its tail as it looked up at him and seemed to nod to the inner door which Patrick knew led into the living room.

Patrick could hear moaning, he thought it sounded like a woman. The dog continued to wag its tail as if he knew what was happening.

He crossed the room and pulled the inner door towards him. The moaning turned into a scream, He opened the door wider and with a shock he saw a female lying on the chaise longue. She was totally naked with her legs in the air, and his son very busy between them. He was mesmerised by her naked breast he could see with its erect nipple and her legs locked around his son.

He pushed the door too in shock, knowing they had been too busy to have seen or heard him. He was sure the dog was smiling, but he ignored it and got out of the cottage as quickly as he could. He could not get the thought out of his head of her breast; in all the time he had been married to his wife she had never let him see hers.

Who was the woman? He did not know her and could not remember being introduced to her. What was all the moaning and screaming about? His wife had never made those noises when he used to make love to her, but then it had been a long time ago since she had allowed him near her. Suddenly he had a strong urge and wondered if he went back into the house whether she would unlock her door. But then again, he knew she wouldn't.

He went to the stables and saddled a black stallion. Today was not the day for his carriage. He wanted to travel fast through the fields and perhaps later he would go to the coffee house and see what took place up those stairs.

It was past noon when Robert walked into the office in the new factory with a big grin on his face. His father was working at a desk checking on some time sheets. He looked up at his son, but found it embarrassing to talk to him. He had a vision in his mind of the scene that he had witnessed that morning.

His son, the grin turning into a big smile, announced that he was going to get married and it was going to be in the Registry Office in three weeks time. Patrick did not know what to say, but he was thankful after what he had seen that morning, at least in his mind that was the right action for his son and heir.

Feeling very uncomfortable, and not knowing where to start a conversation he stood up saying, "I think I will go to the coffee house." As he stood up he could see across the factory floor from the elevated glass fronted office. "Do you know what that group over the far side are discussing? Have we got a problem with production?" He had turned and was looking at Robert.

"That group has nothing to do with production father. But we do have a problem. They have been listening to the tales from the slate quarries in North Wales, where the workers have gone on strike for better working and living conditions. They have not done any work for many months, with the result that a couple of the quarries have had to close down. The tall one with the glasses - he goes by the name of Tibet, he is stirring up trouble. It all started when we finished the house, he is going around comparing where they live to our home. He wants to replicate the miners and call a strike, I am in the mind of sacking him, and I was going to bring it up later."

"What is wrong with their homes?"

"You really don't know. Most of them are slums with no running water and their properties are in a terrible state, leaking roofs and that sort of thing."

"Yes - I saw something similar in the street where Thomas was living when I went and picked him up and brought him back to Mabel."

Patrick went back to the desk and picked up the telephone, flicking the receiver trying to attract the operators' attention. Finally he was put through to his architects and it was Clayton who answered.

"Hello Clayton - Patrick here, I hope you are not very busy?"

"Good day to you Sir. Why - what can we do for you?"

"I understand our work forces in the factory are living in slums with no running water. I want you please to inspect their living accommodation as quickly as possible, and make out a report and deliver it to my office in the city."

"How many properties are we talking about?"

"I do not know, a few hundred I expect. I will get Robert to call round to your office with a list. Please can you do it as soon as possible? In the report I want it to show what is required to bring these places up to a decent standard. I'll pass the phone to Robert so that you can arrange a meeting between you."

When Robert had stopped talking to the Architect, Patrick said, "You had better get the trouble maker up here and any of his friends, it would be better with more than one.

Explain to them what we intend doing to bring their homes up to a living standard, and explain to them that the company will pay for the work"

"Father, if we undertake to do what you ask it is going to cost us a fortune." He spoke quickly with surprise on his face.

"So would a strike which could destroy us. If you need me I will be in my office later in the day." He turned to leave.

"Father, sometimes you seem to forget that I am in charge of the running of Dauntless. So why are you dictating what we should do?"

"Thank you for reminding me son. But the one thing that you have forgotten is that I have shares in the company. Not as many as yours I accept, but as I remember that was a gift from me and also please do not forget it is mostly my money which supports it. My opinion is based on experience which one day hopefully you will have. In the mean time, please do not question my judgement and I do not want to hear that you are in charge again."

Robert sitting at the desk said "Sorry father it won't happen again. I will do what you ask." There was a little pause while Patrick stood there looking at him with his top hat on and holding his walking cane in his hand. "Bye. See you later father. Oh and by the way you left the outside door open this morning in your rush to leave. The dog went out for a run on his own"

Patrick turned, "Is she the woman you are going to marry?"

"Ooh no! That was Molly. She is a bit of fun certainly not the marrying type or one that I would marry! I will bring my prospective bride round home at the weekend – actually you know her- it is Cecil's daughter Mary. I will arrange something with mother."

"Oh I'm pleased. I knew you were friends but not that close." Turning, he started to walk towards the stairs with the vision of the mornings' event and the picture of that naked girl firmly in his mind. He stopped and turned round and sat down again. "How is the new designer progressing?"

"He has settled in well, likable fellow. Very shortly we could have a design for our first four wheeled Dauntless."

"That would be good news. Let me know as soon as he is finished .I'd like to see it."

Leaving the factory Patrick went straight to his office above the Dauntless showroom. He was greeted by his secretary Clara with a hearty "Good morning Patrick." She was sitting at her desk in a separate office to his. Smartly dressed, she was wearing a long tight navy blue coloured skirt and a white blouse buttoned up at the neck. Max is here in your office and he has your messages." Thanking her, he went into his room.

Death for a Starter

Max stood up, as he normally did, to greet Patrick and moved round to the opposite side of the desk. Patrick sat down with his back to the window and looked through the letters that had been opened. One of them was still fastened and was in a wax sealed envelope addressed to him and marked private with a rubber stamp imprint marked 'The War Office.'

Patrick looked at it on the desk. Max said, "That looks interesting." Patrick picked it up and turned the envelope around in his hand, whilst nodding his head.

The letter inside the envelope informed him that a senior member of the Government would be visiting Dauntless on the following Thursday. He would be arriving at Lime Street station at about 1800 hours. He would require transport to collect him from the station, and would the company also please arrange overnight accommodation, for the visitor who they expected to stay two days.

Patrick was a little surprised by the letter, so he wrote a reply to the sender acknowledging their requirements. He called out for Clara, who answered by coming into his office. He passed the reply to her, asking her to write it out in her neat hand, after which she should seal it and send it by courier that same day.

He stood at the window looking at the outside traffic, feeling excitement over the enquiry and yet he could not shake off the terrible low feeling that he had. His office window was opposite a tall building and he often wondered what went on there. On the corner of the road was a man selling hot chestnuts from a steel oven on wheels, shouting his wares. There was a couple he was watching strolling along arm in arm and the thought crossed his mind that his wife had never held his arm. Suddenly he felt very lonely. He knew things would not be the same with his son getting married - another one of his children taking on the responsibility of a family, which would mean he would be less involved in their lives. He felt that he was going to miss the leisure time that they spent together.

He turned from the window and saw that Max was busy answering letters. "I'll be on my way. I have a busy day ahead of me."

"Anything I can do?"

"No not really." He knew it was not quite the truth that he had told Max but he had nothing to do and he was tired and wanted to shake this low feeling.

"There are a few properties that I want you to look at. Shall I arrange it for a few days time?"

"Yes please do. Let me have the details and send them up to the house for me to look at."

"You haven't forgotten the meeting with the accountants on Friday, have you?"

"No that should be interesting - they are always saying we are growing too fast and to pull back. By the way have they sent the figures as yet?"

"Yes they are in my desk. What do you want to do with the cottage overlooking the Mersey? It has plenty of land and I know of a farmer whose son would love to have it to work as a farm."

"I thought you sold it to me so I would have somewhere to go and hide and relax?"

"Yes you are right. Why don't you think about it? The money is good."

Shrugging his shoulders, Patrick said "Yes I'll do that and see you tomorrow."

Putting his outdoors clothes on he thought he would find some company at the coffee house, whilst wondering would he dare to go up those stairs. In order to get to them there was now a door in the main room which he had opened a long time ago, but promptly shut it when a chorus of 'we know where you're going' sprung up from the others in the bar.

Clara his secretary was busy writing in her beautiful longhand, as he walked through saying "Good day, I'll see you tomorrow." He got to the door when he had a sudden thought. "Clara, do you sleep in the same room as your husband?" My God he thought to himself 'what the hell made me ask that' as he felt himself blushing with embarrassment.

She was looking at him in astonishment.

He said before she answered, "I'm sorry, that came out not the way I meant it, and I'll be on my way." Wondering to himself if he would ever be able to face her again.

"Sir! That was a funny question? But you see the question does not arise as I'm not married. If I were I would probably at this moment be at a kitchen sink, instead of sitting here writing your letters. Good day, Sir."

Whatever was coming over him? He was constantly thinking about sex. He had not had these thoughts before. Retrieving his mount from the stables to the rear of the offices, he made his way along the High Street and then turned to go through the market. One of the company's' employees was busy at the Cormack stall and he looked up and waved as he rode past. Patrick acknowledged him by lifting his hand and smiling.

The coffee house was as busy as ever with smoke from the pipes and cigarettes along with lots of laughter above the constant talking. A scream could be heard from one of the ladies on the floor above. From the back rooms where the gaming tables were, came a cheer as someone had won some money. A few of the regulars called out to him. He was thinking to himself he had become very popular since the Dauntless' showroom had opened.

There was a man who was one of the regular fiddlers on the small stage, accompanied by a pretty girl singing.

Patrick was looking at her low cut gown and the swell of her breasts above the material.

He ordered a strong coffee from one of the serving wenches. He found himself staring at her as she went to do his bidding. Patrick turned to the newspaper and tried to concentrate on the news print. The coffee arrived and he held it in his hand, sipping it and looking at the singer, whilst letting his eyes make their way over her body. She was swaying on the stage and twisting so that her skirt which was normally below the knee would flare up, exposing more of her legs. She was also bending forward exposing the swell of her breasts, with her hands making provocative gestures across her body.

Suddenly their eyes locked and she was smiling at him whilst nodding her head towards the door. He felt strange for a moment as if there was nothing else in the world but the two of them. His heart was pounding and he was tempted to take her up on her offer. But the memory of the one and only time he had ventured to do that was too strong - the laughter of it still was ringing in his head. Patrick knew he could not do it.

He turned his head away from the stage with some difficulty, feeling short of breath. He was relieved, and yet a deep feeling of jealousy arose as he saw a man stagger up from where he was seated a few tables away - spilling some of the beer still left in the glass on the table, as he went over to the stage and dragged the singer by her arm, towards the stairwell.

Death for a Starter

Patrick had, had enough and nodded to the serving girl, asking her to arrange for his steed to be brought to the front. In the street the lamp lighters were leaning their ladders against the gas lamps opening their fronts and lighting the elements, giving a gentle glow to the buildings. The stalls in the market place were still busy and the owners had lit oil lamps to give a yellow light to help to see what they were doing.

Patrick was tired as the hangover from the previous nights drinking had not completely worn off. Hence he was going to have a gentle ride home. His wife would probably be out or in her quarters. Robert had a lady friend, so he thought it is going to be earlier than usual, but he might as well retire. What he did not know was that, that decision was going to change his life.

The house seemed to be very quiet. He was told by the butler that madam had taken all the family into Liverpool to the theatre. Patrick thanked him and told him he was going to retire for the night.

"I apologise Sir but I do not think the beds have been turned down, I'll organise it straight away. As I said I am sorry about it but we have some members of staff who are not very well" Patrick then remembered his wife talking about the event in Liverpool, which had been very well publicised which she had wanted to go to. '*She will want to know where I have been all day and was not been here to escort her*'.

Death for a Starter

He turned and went into his office, pressing one of a group of buttons on a consul so that the staff in the servant's quarters would become aware that the Butler required one of them. Patrick was thinking to himself, *'Why do I need the bed turning down - once upon a time the bed was not even made when I got in it let alone turned down.'*

The small room he had taken Benjamin into all those months previously was where any mail or messages for him were deposited. He went in and looked at the list, deciding it could all wait until the morning. He made his way to his suite.

The house seemed so empty without the family. Normally there would have been other sounds as people moved around or spoke to each other. In the background there would have been the sound of music as his daughter practised playing the violin. But it was all strangely silent.

He reached his own drawing room feeling very tired. Normally, in his dressing room his Valet would have had a bath filled with warm water waiting for him. But today everything seemed to be different, but maybe that was because he was earlier than usual. He turned the faucet on and waited for the tub to fill and to get to the right temperature. He undressed, putting his clothes into a wicker basket, where they would be collected and taken to the laundry room the following day.

At last he was luxuriating in the hot water, he could not wait to go to bed, and refresh his tired body. Stepping out of the water, he dried himself vigorously with a warm white fluffy towel. Feeling hot and invigorated from the bath, he slipped into an equally white robe. He was feeling frustrated, but that was not unusual after a hot bath. But then he thought perhaps it is something to do with the events of the past twenty four hours.

There was a noise, which he recognised as somebody being in the adjoining bedroom. Entering the room, he was surprised to see a slim girl in a maid's uniform of long black skirt and white blouse. She was leaning over the bed and starting to turn the top covers over. Her back was towards him. For a moment he was mesmerised as he had not been expecting her. Then he realised it was Ida.

He could feel his heart beating faster. He felt light headed. '*What was it about this woman that made him feel this way?*' He dismissed the thought from his head. There was this strong urge mounting in him.

Suddenly he felt physically powerful and full of energy - the tiredness disappearing. His whole body was quivering with excitement and he could feel the lust rising in him. He crossed the room with only one thought in mind. '*It will be easy to drop her skirt - hadn't he helped to design their uniform? It was only held up by a large bow at the back.*' He crossed the polished floor of the room in bare feet.

The girl heard him coming, but her training as a maid was not to look at the owner. She carried on with what she was doing. She could feel him getting closer and could not understand what he wanted.

Death for a Starter

Suddenly, he was touching her, pushing her further down on the bed. He had his hand on her back. A stroke of fear went through her as she realised what he sought. She had often dreamed of this moment but not like this. She could feel him undoing the tie at her back – she was tempted to scream and run, at the same time realising that was not an option. She would be flung out on the streets, better to let it happen. She felt her skirt sliver down her legs. He was holding her by the hips and then his hardness and a sharp pain, after which a feeling of acceptance flooded through her.

It was over very quickly. He moved away from her, horror flooding through him as he realised what he had done. He sat down in a chair, trying to cover himself, as if now it mattered.

Ida stood up turning around; she bent her knees and gathered up her clothing pulling it up to her waist, reaching behind her to refasten the bow at her back. He watched her and despite what he had done, he could not help admiring her body.

Tears were streaming down her face as she stood up. She was looking at him whilst fiddling with the corner of the white apron pinned around her waist. "What if I am with child - will I be sent to the work house?"

For some reason it was not what he had expected, and then again he did not know what to expect. He realised he was in trouble if the episode got out and became common knowledge.

"Would you be certain it was mine?"

"Sir - I have never been with a man before."

"Yes...yes I think I know. Your name is Ida – isn't it?"

In Patrick's mind he was forming a plan as he remembered the conversation he had had with Max the previous day. A few months previously he had bought a small cottage. It had crossed his mind at the time that it could be somewhere where he could copy what most of the members in the club were doing, but he did not have the slightest idea how to go about it. And now here she was standing right in front of him.

"Yes Sir - if madam finds out I will be put out on the street."

"Then she must not find out, and I think it would be for the best if what I have done, stayed between you and me."

"Yes, Sir."

"I should not have assaulted you. What and why I did, I don't know. You are a lovely woman and I have been attracted to you since you first came here and I think you have felt the same. I am an honourable man and I will protect you." He thought to himself, '*What I have just done brings my honour into question.*' "By the way - where is my Valet?"

"A lot of the staff are very sick with fever, including him. Some of the maids are too, and have taken to their beds."

"Oh I see. That is why you are here."

"It seems I was the only one available."

She stood beside the bed, not moving except for bending over as she wiped the tears from her face with the corner of the apron which she wore around her waist. She looked at him and waited for him to continue.

"If you agree, tomorrow you will leave here. I have a house where you can live and I will pay you a sum of money on a regular basis; all I ask is that from time to time you allow me to visit you. Do you agree?" He was speaking whilst being quietly embarrassed by what he was asking.

She walked slowly across the floor wondering if he was serious. She knelt down in front of him, her eyes sparkling with a tear running down her cheek. "I don't know what to say, Sir."

"You have no need to say anything." He was smiling at her, whilst his brain whirled around looking at all the possibilities. As far as he could remember the next day was clear with no appointments. But if there were any he would cancel them, what was important was to whisk this girl away as soon as possible before she has the time to talk to her friends. "Can you, at midday tomorrow, leave the house and walk towards town?"

"I think so, that is when we normally get the dining room ready for the one o'clock meal."

"All right." Tomorrow leave the house and just keep walking. You had better leave your things here. I will come along and pick you up, if you cannot make it, then try the following day. It is important that nobody sees you leaving the house."

The arrangement was made between them and the next day he had her installed in a large farm house on the outskirts of Liverpool overlooking the Mersey. The property he had bought as an investment some time previously. Although it had crossed his mind at the time, that perhaps he could find a better use for it.

That night he slept soundly with erotic dreams and a feeling of excitement for the morrow.

Chapter Thirty Nine

The thunder was rolling around the heavens after the flash of lightening had lit the dark afternoon sky. The intense rain had started earlier that morning and had got steadily worse. It was now beating heavily on the roofs, the courtyard was flooded in water, which was trying to run away out through the entrance way - but some of it was seeping under the doors, into the house.

Clementine was bored, she had wanted to do some work outside. Instead they were in the drawing room with a log fire crackling away and flames roaring up the chimney, even then the room still felt damp. She and Josh had discussed it many times but they still had not considered what to do with the property. Although they had made a decision to sell the land they owned in Ireland, they had also instructed an Agent to deal with that side of the problem.

"Josh? I am sick and tired of going through these figures. Pounds shillings and pence, they are so difficult to understand, can we convert them into dollars and cents? What's more, I am tired of this strange land and I want to go back home. I do miss Dad"

Death for a Starter

"Sis, you know we cannot change the currency. Persevere with it I'm sure you will work it out. Yes, you are right, I miss our friends in New York as well"

"I have got an idea- with all this rain we cannot do anything outside as we planned, so why don't we have that old trunk brought up from the cellar? – It could be interesting to open it."

"What about the accounts you are looking at?"

"The ones I have gone through seem to be in order. We seem to be spending a lot of money – but if someone is cheating then I cannot see it."

Josh, sighing put the book down which he had retrieved from the house library. He rose up out of the comfortable chair, and pulled the bell rope near the fireplace.

The butler answered their call and came into the room."James, do you remember when you first showed us around the house – there was an old trunk in the cellar, which you said had not been opened for a long time."

"Yes Sir. Oh, and my name is John." He said in a haughty voice. He went on. "It belonged to your father's brother, Major Curtis Evens. He was with the Army in India where he was killed. When it arrived here madam did not want to open it, and it has never been touched from that day to this - she said she had suffered enough and wanted to forget."

Death for a Starter

"Thank you Ja...John. Would you please have it brought up here."

In due course the trunk was brought into the room, the outside of which had been cleaned removing the dirt and cobwebs which had accumulated over the years.

Clementine walked around the item, "There are two padlocks- where are the keys?" At that moment there was a crash of thunder and the house shook.

Josh said, "Sis, I don't think the Gods want you to open it."

"Madam ordered them to be thrown away." The Butler was looking down and was embarrassed although he could not think why.

The locks were broken by one of the gardeners who was called into the drawing room for that purpose. After the workman had left Clementine got down on her hands and knees and with excited anticipation, fervently fiddled with the two buckles on the heavy leather straps, unfastening them.

Looking up a little disappointed she said, "There is nothing here, but...would he have been my Uncle?" She was still on her haunches before continuing, "His uniform and things...this will interest you Josh, a sword." Josh was not taking much notice still interested in the book he was reading, he replied "We will take it home and hang it on the office wall."

Death for a Starter

"Josh! There is something important here in these letters. They are from a Private Detective, name of Harley....look Josh come over here and see what he has to say. It seems the person who murdered....what relation would he have been?"

"Granddad!"

"Oh, of course." She sat thinking still leaning over the box with one finger on her lip. She continued, "They stole his money and then bought his estate from his wife. Perhaps she paid to have him killed?"

Josh looked up from his reading with a sigh, "That is a bit farfetched Sis."

"Well come over here and look at these letters, and see what you think."

**

Despite the weather, a few miles away Patrick was in his favourite black carriage, the rain pouring down and dripping off the roof. He was driving slowly up the road, looking out for the girl, Ida. The thunder and lightning was making the horse jittery. At one stage he had to stop the vehicle and get down to passively calm the animal. The water was running off its back and dripping from the harness.

He had not gone very much further when he saw her sheltering under a tree. She was soaking wet, her woollen cloak clinging to her form. Her face partially hidden by the

Death for a Starter

soft hat she was wearing. Her face was wet, water dripping off her chin. She was shivering with the cold.

There was another clap of thunder as he stopped next to her. He opened the door, with a feeling of excitement held out his hand and helped her into the cold comfort of the four wheeled carriage. She sat on the soft leather seat, water ran from her wet clothes forming pools around her feet and on to the floor. Patrick flicked the reins' and they were off at a brisk pace.

She looked up at him, her wet face trying to smile, "Are we really going to a farm house."

"It will be exactly as I told you yesterday. In the last few hours I have had the place got ready for you. I have also sent somebody on ahead, to light the fires and to get the place warm. They will also have brought some food with them."

They arrived at the property he had bought as an investment a few months previously. But now he recognised what he had been really thinking of, and he remembered Max saying '***Well I would have thought a busy man like you would want somewhere to get away from it all and relax.'*** **He had seen it** as a dream, somewhere he could be alone - possibly with someone warm and nice. And now it was a reality.

He lead the rig into a barn, where he allowed the horse to feed. In one of the stalls there was another pony and a two wheeled trap parked to one side. "Is there someone else here?" she asked.

Death for a Starter

Pointing to the other means of transport he answered, "No they have gone – but that is for your use."

She was speechless and looked on in astonishment. A little while later having refreshed themselves they were sitting in the living area, now his dream had come true. Patrick felt embarrassed; he did not know what to say. She felt the same and was smiling at him. He was wondering how his friends from the club, started a conversation? He could not get over his embarrassment. He was tempted to lead her into the bedroom, but then what? He would not know what to do.

Patrick stood up and the girl looked up at him. He said, "Make yourself comfortable – it is your place. A housekeeper will join you on Monday to help with the chores. It is now your home so it will be up to you where she stays. But I do not want her around when I come and visit."

"There is no need, Patrick." On the journey to her new home she had got used to calling him by his Christian name.

"Can you handle the pony and trap."

"Yes I think so."

He was taking out his wallet and extracting money from it, "You will need some clothes and things. Here take this and go into town and get what you want."

"Thank you. When will I see you again?"

He picked up his cloak. She looked disappointed. "I don't think there is anything else. I will be off now, and I'll

Death for a Starter

come back in a couple of days. I think Tuesday would be the right time." Before she could reply he was gone.

That night he was feeling a little foolish why hadn't he done more, perhaps at least kissed her, he had not realised how embarrassed he would feel. It had all felt so clinical, somehow he would change that and his thoughts of how to do it, gave him a feeling of excitement and he was looking forward to his return to the farm house.

Chapter Forty

It was the following day when the storm had passed, and Ida could not wait to show off her new toy. Shortly after breakfast she went into the barn and attached the pony to the small trap.

She had one thought in mind and that was to go to her old rented house, collect some things and to spend some time with her old friends.

She guided the vehicle into the narrow street and was greeted by people that used to be her friendly neighbours. "What have you had to do to get that Ida?" Some shouted, followed by other suggestive remarks.

Ida was upset she had thought her old friends would have been pleased for her, instead she realised there was a certain amount of jealousy. Stopping outside her old living quarters, Wiley was standing in the doorway, "So what have you got there, girl?"

"Never you mind. Have you been paying the rent?"

Death for a Starter

"I had to sell some of your things to do that. Anyway I want to know where you got that?" pointing to the rig.

Ida then realised her mistake in coming back here, and she could not wait to get away again.

Wiley was not going to be put off, "I bet you had to lay on your back to get it. Some fancy man was it?"

"It has nothing to do with you and what right did you have to sell my things?" She had raised her voice and was staring at him. A crowd had gathered round not wanting to miss what otherwise was a normal boring day.

Ida turned around in time to see one of the kids trying to lead the pony away. Grateful she had thought to apply the brake to the small vehicle. She shouted at the boy, "Leave it alone, you rascal."

This brought more cheering from the on lookers. Holding her bag close to her, which contained the money Patrick had given her. She knew what the neighbours were like and was frightened that somebody would snatch it from her. Hastily climbing back onto the small cart picking up the reins and flicking the pony's back with them, she was off, with more cheers and rude remarks from the people that used to be her friends.

The rest of the day she spent shopping in the stores in Liverpool, looking forward to the next visit from her new friend, she was determined to make him happy and to keep him.

Chapter Forty One

Robert was having difficulty with the work force. He had invited them to a meeting as his father had suggested, to see if he could calm the fervour which was building up over living conditions. Although Robert had explained that the Architect had been instructed to view their homes, to determine what was required and to bring them up to a comfortable living standard. It had done little to quell the anger of some of the men.

Tibet, who could read and write, had fallen on hard times a few years before. He had lived in decent houses in Liverpool before his downfall, because of that, everybody recognised him as the leader of the group. He was very forceful when he spoke, "It is all very good telling us all this rubbish, it does not alter the fact that my wife and family are living in a dirty hovel." The other group of five men were murmuring in agreement.

Death for a Starter

Robert was taken aback by the anger in his words, "We understand the situation, which I may add was not of our making but we intend to change it. May I remind you, all of you lived in those places before being employed by Dauntless? Tomorrow we will determine what is required to bring the homes up to standard." His words did not go down well with the workforce.

"How do we know you are not just fobbing us all off, eh?" Again there were murmurs of approval.

"I can assure you all we are not – we want to resolve this problem. As I said tomorrow you will find a team of men visiting your homes to look for what improvements need to be done. You should advise each of your wives' to expect them."

"And who is going to pay for all this?"

"As I have already explained when I invited you to this meeting, which of course is in the firm's time, and not yours" He added sarcastically. "Patrick has already authorised it, and the firm wants your living accommodation to be brought up to an acceptable level and Dauntless Industries will pay. That is of course if there is no interruption in production. After the team has visited your homes tomorrow, builders will be instructed to carry out what work is required"

One of the group spoke up saying, "We have heard what he has got to say, we will see if he is telling the truth when tomorrow comes."

Death for a Starter

After some more murmurings and a threat of downing tools if what he was implying did not happen, the group disbursed.

The following day Clayton with a list in his hand was working his way through the various hovels, where the Dauntless workers lived. In most cases the roads outside were no more than dirt tracks with open drainage. The floors inside the dwellings were not much different. The women trying to make a home out of these shelters, themselves poorly dressed, and were not very responsive as they showed the Architect their living quarters.

As the team trailed around from home to home, they were being followed by small children in various modes of dress, but mostly dirty and in rags all asking for payouts. Clayton with measuring devices and with the help of one of his staff was determining what would be required, to bring these cold leaking homes up to some form of standard. Trying to ignore the cries of the babies where they lay in make do cots surrounded by poor sanitation.

The two of them took three days to complete their survey of more than a hundred properties, in some cases listening to rude remarks from the occupiers, always feeling uncomfortable in their surroundings. By the end of the work, Clayton had a sheet of paper for each one, with a sketch of the layout, and a brief summary of what was required to remedy the poor living conditions.

Death for a Starter

He returned to his office, depressed and feeling dirty from the scruffy homes. He put the list detailing the work needed into numerical order and then into a folder, with the Clayton and Partners name emblazoned in gold leaf on the front. The fronts cover also had particulars of the project and an estimate of the cost.

Satisfied with the result he telephoned Patrick at his office above the showroom. Clara answered informing him that her boss was at the railway station meeting guests from London, but nevertheless she could arrange a meeting for them, which they agreed should take place in a few days time.

All this had taken too long and the men in the factory were not happy. Tibet had demanded to see Robert, "You told us last week that you were taking action to improve our living standard. Nothing appears to have taken place except for a 'Nancy boy' walking around taking measurements."

Robert was annoyed but he did not want to show it. Sitting on the high stool behind the elevated sloping desk, he looked up smiling from the paper work he was involved in. "Tibet…you are a very clever man and should be able to go places – you must also understand that these things take time – drawings have to be completed and then decisions made, of how to proceed. I promise you we will involve all of you, when it is time and we know what is involved."

"What decisions – not to do the work I bet! And are you trying to bribe me with your offer of going places…let me tell you that will not wash with me…oh I know your sort…"

Death for a Starter

"Enough, before you say something we will both regret." Robert turned back to the desk and continued what he was doing, also saying, "I think it would be better if you were to go back to what you were doing. In the mean time I will talk to the Architect and see what progress there is and then I will let you know."

Tibet went to speak. But Robert spun round very quickly, the other could see he was getting angry, "I said that is enough...I will tell you very shortly what is happening." The employee left murmuring to himself.

**

Patrick, after some deliberation had decided to go alone to meet the London train. He told the driver, who was sitting on the high seat controlling the twin horses, to park the black shining carriage in the wide road adjacent to the train terminal.

He walked into the station and on to the platform, watching the train arriving belching steam and smoke as it made its way slowly along the side of the passenger area. He had a description of the man he was meeting, recognising him immediately as he alighted from the first class carriage, wearing a long brown coat, as Patrick had expected. However he was surprised when two other men joined the first.

The owner of Dauntless walked towards them with confidence, holding his hand out at the same time, saying, "Pleased to meet you Sir, my name is Patrick Cormack. I have

Death for a Starter

a carriage waiting for you." He was nodding his head in the direction of the road. He was thinking to himself he was glad he had brought the larger vehicle, it would have been embarrassing if the vehicle he was in only had two seats.

The newcomer was speaking, "My name is Fitch – Edward Fitch very pleased to be here and to meet you Mr Cormack. We have heard a lot about you - Cormack is that Irish?" He looked Patrick in the eye.

Suddenly Patrick felt belittled and he did not like the feeling. He could see one of the other men collecting cases from the train. He tried to sound convincing when he said. "Yes Mr Fitch. Is that a problem? You see my family have lived here a long time and built two businesses from scratch. In fact I was only a boy when we first arrived."

"Well it is something that will have to be considered. Can we first of all go to the manufacturing plant. We would like to see the facilities for producing the machines?" They walked on a few paces before saying. "Is there somewhere we can dine? We would like to have a meal first. There was nothing on the train." Patrick knew exactly where he would take them, to the Atlas club, which would impress them.

Whilst at the table the man from the Ministry explained, "We have without your knowledge, had one of your motorcycles on trial- of course amongst others. In some cases they are more superior to horses – but we cannot see the day when they will replace them."

Death for a Starter

"Thank you Sir that is encouraging."

"The Minister for War who is responsible for these things has indicated that if what we see here, over the next few days is up to a high standard, then we would like you to come to London to discuss the purchase and maintenance of a fleet of your machines, for use by the armed forces."

After a sumptuous meal and further discussion at the Club, Patrick explained that he had other pressing matters, if they would excuse him he would leave them in the very capable hands of Robert, the chief executive of Dauntless Motorcycles, who would be very pleased to show them the workings of the company.

After the three men left the Club with Robert they resumed their journey to the manufacturing plant. All four of them were surprised to find the workforce gathered around in a group being addressed by one of the men. What they could not hear was the speaker was trying to convince the men to strike until work on their homes as promised, had started.

The man from London asked what they were doing. Robert as quick as a flash said, "They are voting on a proposal by the company to improve their living conditions."

"And why would they want to do that. Surely if you are agreeing to improve their lives why would they want to vote on it?"

Robert was thinking quickly he did not want the people from London to think they had a problem, "I think they are deciding whose house should be done first." Knowing the design department was not involved in the meeting he suggested, "Would you like to see the Design Office, it is where we plan for the future?" Feeling stupid at the statement *'what else would a design department do.?'*

Following their agreement he instructed the coachman to go to the far side of the building where there was a separate entrance.

Chapter Forty Two

Josh and Clementine were seated in front of their lawyer. Josh was speaking, "But don't you see Alfred – this letter says it all?"

By this time the two of them after many meetings, and dealings with him over the estate they were inheriting, both the Americans were on Christian names terms with their lawyer.

"Yes I see your meaning Josh, but it was a long time ago. We would need proof and something tangible, that these events took place. After all, at the time this letter could be some sort of scam, to someone a long way away. Also we must remember we are talking about a very wealthy family, with strong connections. Whatever we do it will not be easy."

Death for a Starter

Clementine interrupted, "What sort of proof? If need be, I do not mind going to Ireland to see what I can find out over there. Surely there must be some records kept by the authorities at the time."

"Clementine, I don't know. A lot has happened in the thirty odd years since this letter was written. I suppose we could start by finding this Harley. I was not involved in the conveyance of the property to the Cormack's, it was my predecessor, and I am afraid he has left us, so there is no help there. I think the place to start, is as I said, to find this Harley. If, as it says, he is a Private Detective, then I have never heard of him, and we hire a few from time to time"

The brother and sister were disappointed with their lawyers' advice, but they were determined to find out if the story in the letters was true, or just some form of prank only understood by the originator.

Chapter Forty Three

Clayton, had arrived at Patrick's office earlier that morning, they were discussing, with Max, the work that was needed to bring the workforce houses up to a decent living environment. The cups were strewn around the table where Clara had supplied them with tea. One by one the sheets in the folder had been studied and an inventory of what was required listed in each unit, on a separate sheet.

"Clayton, I think the next step is to instruct a builder to carry out this work. What do you think?"

"Alright. I know of a firm, who we have used in the past with good results. As you know, the figures are in front of you, it is going to be very expensive. Shall we run through it again to see where we can save money? Because, quite frankly in the state they are in they should all be pulled down. What do you think, Max?"

"Yes...I do agree with you. And I agree we should see how we can save money, but would that mean skimping on the work – if we were to pull them down where would these people live?"

Patrick had been thinking, "Max, on the way back from the Mersey Farm." Clayton looked up sharply - this was the first time he had heard of a Mersey farm. "There is a strip of unused land, it runs close to the river."

Death for a Starter

Max was nodding his head, "Yes I know of it – but what about it?"

"Well I have been thinking – these people must be paying rent on these hovels. Supposing we were to build new houses on that piece of land and rent them to the work force? In the mean time we could make their existing properties more comfortable."

Clayton was nodding his head. "That land is a fair distance from the plant. I know of another piece which is nearer and would be more suitable. But then have you thought of the cost of constructing these houses?"

Patrick replied, "That is the beauty of such a scheme. If we repair the existing and bring them up to standard, it is dead money. But by building new ones we would retain the money in the value of the houses We would also have an income from them in the way of rent."

A little while later the meeting broke up and Clayton left them, while Max and Patrick was left to discuss other matters. But first Max said "I see you are making good use of the Mersey farm?"

"You were right when you sold it to me, somewhere to go and relax. So when we finish here that is where I am heading."

Chapter Forty Four

At the Rose and Crown, the tavern in Huyton, Wiley not daring to be seen in the town, had entered the building during the darkness of the early evening. His two friends had been expecting him, they were seated around a table in an upstairs room waiting for a meal to be served.

"So what are your plans Wiley?" The tall one named John asked.

"Are you referring to the Cormack's? If you are then I thought that was why I am here to go through what action you want taken to get rid of this man?"

"We have some ideas – but we thought we would see what you have in mind?"

"I want him dead and out of my life" He turned round lifting up his shirt, "Look at my back – he did that with a whip

Death for a Starter

– it bloody hurt I can tell you. What did he do to you - just made you walk a few miles back here?"

"It was more than that, Tom here with his gammy leg could hardly walk and finished with bad blisters. He also made us look stupid and robbed us – he took the money we had fairly won off his son."

"Alright we do not want to argue about who is hurt more than the other – let us get on with discussing what we are going to do about it."

Tom, the smaller of the two, spoke, "We thought of burning his house down. Of course while he is inside. We understand the Cormack's workers are up in arms about where they live in respect to their hovels compared with the luxury of his house – so our guess is they would get the blame for it."

At that moment the maid Rose had arrived in the narrow and poorly lit hall with only an oil lamp on to show her the way. She was putting the food she had brought from the kitchen onto a small table. Before knocking on their door, she stopped for a moment listening to the voices on the other side.

"That is interesting Tom - but it is a big place and he would get out before the fire took hold?"

"Not if we use petroleum spirit?"

"What the hell is that?"

"It is the liquid they put into the new type of horseless carriage to make them go. There is a garage on the outskirts of

Death for a Starter

Liverpool that sells it. But mind it is very dangerous because it explodes. The house would disappear in a few seconds."

"You're kidding me?"

"No, we know Wiley – break in, spread it around the floor, and get out before lighting the match – and we mean it, get out don't light it in there."

"But how would we know he is in there?"

"Easy...he goes everywhere in that big black shiny coach. If that is in the coach house he will be at home."

There was a knock on the door. Wiley was thinking and looking at the fire and the logs burning in the grate and he heard Tom saying "Enter."

The girl entered carrying the food tray, she was wearing a white top with a full skirt, as she leant forward putting the serving dishes down on the table, Wiley could see the swell of her breasts beneath the blouse.

"Well, well who have we here" He was looking at the girl.

"Its Rose but I have heard her called Roxy – she works in the kitchen. She's alright."

The three men gathered around the table taking handfuls of food and stuffing it in their mouths. The girl turned round and left.

Death for a Starter

Wiley, with his mouth full of food asked, "Does she sleep in one of the rooms?"

The tall one answered, "I think I know what's on your mind Wiley. Yes she has a room in the attic – she's works with the cook here and that's where the food comes from."

"I'll have a little wager with you two, in a minute."

Tom turned his head to look at Wiley, spitting out food as he asked. "What sort of wager?"

The girl was coming back into the room with jugs of ale as he answered, "You'll see?" Winking at the other two as he said it, at the same time reaching into a wallet strapped to his waist.

Rose put the jugs down on the table in front of them. Wiley took hold of one of her arms with a firm grip. With his other hand he put a half a gold sovereign on the table, which was more money than Roxy had seen in many a month in the work she was doing.

Pointing to the coin Wiley said, "That girl, is for you." She gasped, saying, "Thank you Sir."

The other two were looking on wondering what was going to happen next.

"Ha." He took a long swig of the beer, still holding her arm. "But I want another drink."

Death for a Starter

She tried to pull her arm away, saying, "I'll get it right away for you – Sir."

"Ha yes - but to get the coin, when you come back, you can keep your skirt on but I want to see those lovely little '*titties*' in the flesh." She went red as he let go of her arm and she turned and almost ran to the door.

Wiley was laughing, "Well my friends the bet is this – my half sovereign says she will come in baring her all against your two half sovereigns which says she won't."

John the tall one said, "I'm on, because she is strong willed and money does not seem to interest her – but not being bedded does. You have just done your money." Tom agreed with him and they both covered the bet on the table.

Roxy went to the bar and replenished their glasses. Before returning to the men, she went to her room and changed into her clothes she used in her act, the only difference she left her blouse open to the front. She retrieved the beer and went to their room.

"Where the bloody hell is she? She better not have cried out, I'll find her because if I want a woman then I have her."

Roxy had just arrived at the door when she heard this tirade from Wiley. She checked to make sure her knives were in place and heard a little bit more from the tall one.

Death for a Starter

He was leaning over to pick up the coin he had placed on the table. "I told you, you would lose Wiley."

"Leave the money there I have not finished yet."

"What's the point she has not come back." Tom also wanted the return of his bet. "And the way I see it you owe us half a big one each."

The door opened and Roxy came in carrying three jugs of beer in front of her. They could all see she had changed and was wearing red trousers with gold braid piping with a matching blouse, open to the front exposing her bare flesh. Wiley quickly swiped up the two coins and put them in his wallet. She put the drinks on the table, the three men were mesmerised by her breasts with two erect nipples.

She stepped quickly back from the table, saying, "Wiley, flip that coin over to me."

He laughingly took a swig of the beer some of the froth staying on his beard. "You have not done what I asked - and if you think I am going to give you half a sovereign for me to see your tits, you are wrong - I can go and see a pair anywhere for tuppence." He was getting up and looking menacingly at her.

Tom said, "Wiley, you lost the bet and I want my money back, and I want it now."

"I agree with Tom, give us our money and then we take it in turns with the girl. I knew all along what you where

Death for a Starter

planning - it hasn't changed much instead of just taking off her top it will be great fun taking the other things off her."

They were all getting the worse for drink, Tom was into his beer and spluttering, "Throw a coin on the table if it lands heads up Wiley you can have her first – if it is tails then we will sort it out between us who is going to have the initial joy." He stood up and was undoing the buckle on his thick leather belt holding up his breeches.

"This is my bloody idea and I am not throwing anything on the table, you can sort it out between you who is after me." He shrugged his coat off and took a small gun out of his waist, pointing it at the other two men, and then laying it on the table.

Roxy was still standing with her back to the door a small grin on her face and very happy to let the three men argue amongst themselves. It had not occurred to them that she was standing upright and tall with her legs apart waiting to pounce.

The tall one, John, he was the furthest from the door, and was sitting on the far side of the table, across from Wiley. He got up pushing the chair over in his haste, which landed with a crash on the floor. "She is standing there wiggling her tits at me getting me all excited – enough – you two can watch." He was staggering to the end of the table also undoing his belt, pushing Tom out of the way who was trying to hold him back. Wiley was going for the gun he had previously put on the table.

Death for a Starter

As the tall one rounded the end of the table, still struggling to free himself from his partner, a flicker of light caught the blade as it flashed through the air. It sunk deep into John's chest, blood squirted from the wound as he dropped to the floor.

Wiley spun round to look at Roxy but he was too late she had moved very quickly up behind him, and was now holding a similar knife firmly to his throat. Leaning over she picked up the coin, sliding it into a pocket. Then reaching into his wallet took the remainder of his money. "You see Wiley, when I perform my act in the circus, I frequently do it exposing my breasts - but I get paid far more than you offered." She took the gun - backing away she held it facing the two men. She moved round the end of the table to retrieve her knife. It made a gurgling sound as she pulled it from the tall one's body, wiping the blade on the man's shirt.

Tom thought she was slightly distracted while removing the knife and put his hand into his coat. The little gun spat once and he screamed as the bullet entered his arm.

"Wiley, I am leaving now – but I think you should find a doctor for Tom and your other friend, although I don't think he will be able to do much for the one on the floor." With that she was out of the door, only pausing enough to lock it behind her having changed the key from the inside a lot earlier.

Inside the room they could hear her footsteps as Roxy ran down the hall. Wiley rushed to the door but he knew he

Death for a Starter

was too late as he had heard the key turn in the lock. "Is there another way out – come on we have got to get after her."

"What with a bullet in my arm..."

"That's just a scratch...how do I get out of here – I want to get after that bitch, I'll kill her." He was kicking the door.

"As far as I'm concerned after the demonstration we have just witnessed she is one dangerous person and I don't want to go near her – but you do what you like."

**

Earlier that afternoon, Patrick's first visit after taking Ida to the farm house began. It was a beautiful day with the sun shining on the front of the property. She had been waiting for him and came to the door when she heard his carriage arrive in the yard behind the house. She was leaning against the doorframe, her hands clasped together in front of her giving the impression of coyness. No longer a skirt down to her ankles instead it daringly finished just below the knee. Her blouse was off the shoulder the white of her skin reflecting in the sun light and the gold of her hair in sharp contrast. *'She looks like one of those ladies upstairs in the coffee house.'* Was Patrick's first thought, but trembling and feeling very excited. He had a feeling he would not be as embarrassed as he was when he delivered her to her new home.

They entered the small hallway of the house with its oak beamed ceiling and white plastered walls. She took him

Death for a Starter

by the hand and led him into the living room. She removed his top hat putting it on to a chair. Turning back to him she removed his tailcoat sliding it provocatively down his arms. He was stunned as she pushed him into a chair. Standing in front of him she did a twirl, "Do you like it?" She had a wide grin on her face as she lifted the hem of her skirt, as she said it.

He nearly choked on his words muttering "Lovely."

Ida laughed, "Lovely! Is that all – wouldn't you like to see more?" She leant over putting her hands on her knees, the blouse showing a little more of the soft flesh with the dark shadow in between. "The fire is alight in the bedroom making it very cosy – would you like me to turn the sheets down?" She said laughing. Reminding him of the occasion when he had forced his way with her, which made him feel very uncomfortable and almost destroyed the moment. But then he knew she was teasing and no answer was needed.

The desire for her persisted as it had done since he had set eyes on her all that time ago. He lifted himself out of the chair and followed her. She held the bedroom door open for him, holding her cheek out to him for a kiss.

The touch of her skin was too much he took hold of her and laid her on the bed. She pushed him to one side and laughing said "You are always in such a rush." Her fingers were undoing the buttons on his shirt as she said it.

Death for a Starter

"You told me you had not been with a man before...you seem to be very experienced?"

Suddenly she was holding him, "I have always wanted to do that – I have watched how excited my brothers got when it was done to them."

She was snuggling into his bare chest her tongue flipping across it. She stopped and looked into his eyes, "I told you the truth...but when you live and sleep in the same room as four brothers you see things, especially when they bring girls home...and of course there is your mother and father...err...playing families."

Patrick's mind went back to his childhood and the lack of privacy in the small cottage in Ireland. She continued briefly, "My father sent me away to an uncle who sent me to a school so I could become a lady. And here I am – your lady."

For the rest of the afternoon Ida did things to him, touching, stroking bring his feelings to a crescendo and finally the pure relief of collapsing beside her and letting sleep overtake him. Only to be woken up a short time later as she started to stroke him again and brought the desire, which he thought he had exhausted, back again, as she moved herself on top of him.

It was a lot later when Patrick realised it was getting dark and long shadows were creeping across the window, and with reluctance he got up kissing her on the cheek as he did so. His overwhelming thought was that he had to see this woman again, and it seemed to him that once a week would not be enough. The thought crossed his mind *'why not come and live here?'*

Chapter Forty Five

C

Clementine and Josh had been referred to a senior legal person who was interested in their situation. He was reading the old document that had been sent to their Uncle Curtis. She wanted to say something of what they had found out so far – but he held his hand up to stop her as he continued to read underlining parts of the text with a pencil.

She looked at her brother and shrugged her shoulders, after which she looked around the room admiring the decor of wood panelling while they waited for the senior solicitor to put the pencil down and talk to them.

"You say you found this letter in a trunk?"

"Yes – it was stored in the cellar."

Death for a Starter

"Who was it addressed to?"

Josh was getting frustrated; they had explained all this before. "The trunk was still sealed - it had been sent from India and the contents belonged to our Uncle Curtis who we know joined the Army around about that time. If there had been a letter with it we do not know where that is. But without doubt that is where it came from and contained our uncles' belongings."

"And the letter? Looking at it could be somebody's idea of a joke. Was it sealed....?"

Clementine spoke a little harshly. "It had been opened and was in the package which had been sent from this city Liverpool – it also had a date when it was sent. We have been making enquiries and we have been to Ireland - it all appears to match up – there was an O'Dowd small holding in Ireland where my Grandfather was killed. A child by the name of Patrick lived there. There is a church in Tullamore and the Priests over the years have kept perfect records. There is a large ledger which we were allowed to see – about fifty years ago there was a marriage between Reuben O'Dowd and a Florence Cormack – later they had a child called Patrick who was baptised there. But the address for the marriage is quite different from the one where the O'Dowd's lived...but the Cormack's built a house and called it Tullamore. We went to Dublin Castle and there they searched through their records of the time, they were looking for this family with the name of O'Dowd, but could not find any trace of them. There was a

Death for a Starter

note on the file to say they believed that they had emigrated to England."

Josh added, "In that period no records were kept of people travelling between Ireland and England...but there are too many coincidences that the Patrick that lives in what used to be our property, is one and the same person"

"Are you suggesting it is the same Patrick that lives at the Cormack farm – that is a bit farfetched there must be thousands of Patricks?"

With a sigh Josh said, "Yes...yes that is exactly what I am saying."

His sister took up the conversation, "We know there must be thousands of Patricks it is a very common name - but when you look at the other facts in the document it does not appear to be so farfetched – as you put it." She had pointed to the paper on the desk.

The legal man snorted. "What are you asking me to do?"

Clementine was on the verge of stamping her feet, "We thought you would tell us what to do – the information in that letter explains everything –our grandfather was killed and robbed and we believe there was some conspiracy to obtain the farm out of grandmother. And we want it back"

The elderly man leaned back in his chair and taking off his monocle rubbed his eyes, with a pristine white

Death for a Starter

handkerchief he had removed from an inner pocket. He picked up the old letter once more, glancing through it trying to formulate some advice for these two people. "My thoughts are, it is really a police matter. But what they can do after all these years, is in my opinion very little. If you wish I could write to this ...err...Patrick Cormack - pointing out your concerns and see what reaction that brings?"

The brother and sister had expected more and looked at each other with resignation on their faces. Clementine spoke. "Thank you if you would do that and as you say – we will see what that brings." They stood up shaking the solicitors' hands as they made their way out through the large solid oak door.

"Before you go I do think you are right but proving it would be very difficult. It would be pointed out to us that the whole story is only a suspicion and could just boil down to someone trying to make mischief. But I will see what I can do."

**

Robert and his guests were getting on very well, they had toured the design centre and were very impressed with the company's plans and were fascinated by the drawing which showed the shape of a small sidecar to be attached to the Dauntless motorcycle. They were astonished to understand that a full grown person could sit in it with comfort, and the machine was powerful enough to take the load.

Death for a Starter

By the time they had moved into the factory to inspect the final manufacturing process, the workforce had returned and were busy producing motorcycles. They had a few words with some of the workers and were satisfied that all was well with the personnel, much to Roberts's relief.

Once more he returned the trio back to the Atlas Club House, where Robert expected to see his father, but was disappointed to find that he had not arrived as yet. They were seated in one of the comfortable rooms reserved for guests when Patrick arrived fresh from his afternoon's liaison.

Sitting in a circle in comfortable leather chairs, Robert guided the conversation into what had taken place that afternoon and events at the factory, and the company's plans for the future. The visitors were keen to know as much as possible about the new four wheel version of the Dauntless, which they had also seen on the drawing boards.

Robert explained that it would not be too many weeks before they had a trial version to try out on the test track which was to the rear of the plant.

The leader of the group explained they were very pleased with their visit and they wanted Patrick and Robert to visit London for further discussions of introducing their product to the armed forces. But there was a certain amount of urgency as the Minister was going to South Africa in a few days, as there was trouble brewing with the Boers.

Death for a Starter

"We would appreciate it if you were to bring your wives, We will, as I have indicated be meeting the Minister for War – and sometimes he likes to meet people in an informal manner. He very much likes to get to know the families of the people we are trading with. We hope that will be acceptable to you and your ladies. We will of course provide very comfortable accommodation in one of the best hotels in London?"

Patrick and Robert looked at each other in surprise both were dumbfounded - before the elder answered, "Of course – we will make arrangements for them to travel with us."

"We really need you in London two days after tomorrow – we understand it is very soon but the Minister is going away at the end of the week and he will need to meet you before he goes."

"That may be a bit too soon for the ladies but perhaps they can go another time."

"Yes of course – if they do come we will have made arrangements for them."

Leaving their visitors at the club to make themselves comfortable Patrick and Robert climbed into the large black shiny coach. The coachman encouraged the horses into a trot and they made their way to Tullamore. "Well Robert what do you think of that?"

Death for a Starter

"Certainly a surprise father – but I cannot see mother wanting to go. No way will she miss her bridge club."

"Yes my thoughts exactly. And what about your wife to be – do you think she will want to travel to London if mother does not go?"

"There is another problem I cannot go tomorrow I have another meeting which is important. Why don't you take Max with you?"

As his son was frequently having meetings with clients it did not occur to Patrick to ask why he could not go to London, instead he said, "I will telephone Max when we get home. It is not a bad idea he is very good at keeping notes"

Chapter Forty Six

Wiley was very angry, he stopped kicking the door and turned looking at Tom. He was convinced Roxy would have left and would not be in the building, "Where the bloody hell did you get that woman?"

Tom was feeling feint he was losing a lot of blood, "From an Agency." He mumbled.

"Come on man tell me what Agency." He was grabbing him by the collar.

"It is near the town hall - off the main square."

"And the name?"

Before Tom collapsed across the table, he managed to give Wiley the name and the directions he needed. With the information he wanted he made another attack on the door.

Death for a Starter

Which finally started to splinter as the thin box wood gave way to the pounding it's aggressor was giving it,

The cook was cowering in the kitchen trying to keep the work table between her and the door, as Wiley burst in, "Where did the bitch go?"

She pointed to the door as he walked around the table, she tried to pull away from him in the limited space, "Why didn't you come up and open the door when I was knocking?"

"I was frightened, we have strict instructions not to interfere." He slapped her hard around the face and ran to the door. A moment later he was back, "Where's my horse?"

She was still rubbing her face, "The girl took it, Sir." She tried to turn away from him to no avail, he kicked and slapped her. Before leaving he asked. "Well then, where are the other animals?"

"They'll be in the bottom field." Wiley shouted in frustration and kicked the poor woman again before leaving, ranting and roaring as he did so.

Wiley had a problem, he knew if he went to try and find a horse then it would quickly be known he was back in town. And he did not want that. Remembering what had happened to his accomplices the last time he was in Huyton. He set off walking along the Liverpool Road.

He had walked a few miles from the town, when he saw a horseman a little way ahead coming round a bend. The

Death for a Starter

rider was pushing his mount hard, it was then Wiley realised it was a mail delivery man

Wiley held up his hand asking him to stop. The rider was surprised to see someone out this early in the morning and the thought struck him that maybe he was a highwayman who held up travellers to rob them. He had slowed his mount to stop to see what the stranger wanted. Then changing his mind he encouraged the horse to go past. But the horse refused Wiley was in the way. The rider kicked the horse encouraging it to go forward. The animal reared up throwing the rider. Wiley realised what the rider had intended to do and made a lunge for the horses bridle. The horse spun round, he now had a firm grip on the horses harness. The rider who had fallen heavily onto the road was trying to get up. Very quickly Wiley put one foot into a stirrup and swung over into the saddle, turning the animal in the opposite direction and whipping the horses into a gallop.

**

When Patrick and his son arrived home, they found Victoria had retired to her rooms some time before. Bidding Robert good night, he went into his study, and called Max. On the desk was a rolled parchment sealed with red wax and tied with a pink ribbon. He looked at the sender and saw it was from a very well known law firm in the city, immediately he knew somebody had spent a lot of money to have this document sent to him.

Death for a Starter

Feeling a little nervous he pulled on the ribbon, and then with a paper knife slit the seal. The official document unfurled in front of him. He straightened it out on the desk, smoothing down the corners. Reaching up he adjusted the desk lamp to cast more light on the parchment.

He read slowly through the document and realised that someone had gone to a lot of trouble to put the events almost in their correct order. He was badly shaken and lay back in the chair looking at the ceiling. *'After all this time – all the effort and the wealth he had created – would it all come to nothing?'*

The document was demanding a reply with the view to having a meeting to discuss the matter. But he was not a man who made quick decisions – it looked bad, yes – but it could not get any worse while he slept on it. In the morning he would discuss it with his own lawyers and make decisions after that. One thing for certain he was not going to let it spoil his trip to London, and the accolade that awaited him there, when the Dauntless motorcycle becomes the first mechanised vehicle to be used in the Army.

Patrick was in his small study, which was situated near to the front entrance of the house with a small window overlooking the driveway. Although it was dark outside he saw the shadow of a mounted horse go past. It created a mere pause in his thoughts which were racing around the problem of the document. Rolling it back into its original form he took a key from his pocket, bent over and twirled some knobs and opened the safe below his desk, storing the document there for safe keeping away from prying eyes. In his mind an answer to

Death for a Starter

the accusations was forming in his head – but it would wait until the morning.

The rider he had seen passing the window was Roxy, still in her circus act livery. She guided the horse down the lane beside the large house, and as she had been told, she came to the first small stone cottage, where hopefully Mabel lived.

In one of the downstairs windows there was the light from a flickering oil lamp, and the sound of a baby crying. She dismounted and opening a gate she led her mount into a field opposite her destination. Removing its saddle she returned to the window, and tapped on it.

The baby hearing the noise stopped crying for a moment. She tapped again, and then she heard the unmistakable voice of her friend asking "Who's there?"

"You did say I could come round and see you. So I am here."

"Roxy...what are you doing here at this time of night. Hold on I'll let you in."

As the sound of movement came from the room she moved along to the front door of the property. The door opened with a small squeak from a dry hinge, standing in the opening was Mabel. She was holding an infant in her arms, with the knuckle of one finger in its mouth, which the child was happily sucking on.

Death for a Starter

"My God! Why are you dressed like that? You had better come in. It is a bit dark, but you get used to it - they haven't extended the electricity from the main house to here as yet. Now tell me why you have arrived here in the early hours of the morning – dressed as if you are going on stage."

"It is a long story but I did do part of my stage act."

There was a moan and a shout from upstairs, "I don't know what is going on down there - but would you please be quiet, I have work to do in the morning."

Mabel ushered her friend into the small room of the house, holding one of her other fingers to her lips. "That was Thomas. Don't worry he's alright but he has to get up early." They sat down in two comfortable chairs in the living room, Mabel nursing the baby.

Roxy said "I have come on a horse and have tethered it in the field opposite."

"That will be fine we will get one of the stable lads to find room for it in the stables. But that can wait until the morning. Now tell me what has been happening?" Roxy started to explain the events of the evening and they spent the rest of the night talking.

Chapter Forty Seven

Patrick came down to breakfast which was normally served in the small annex just off the kitchen; he was surprised to find his wife was there before him.

"And can I ask where you were all day yesterday – you did not come in until very late?"

"It was a very busy day, yesterday we had buyers up from London."

"And what is that supposed to mean?"

"It does not mean anything other than I was busy. They were, and are people from Government – they are looking to purchase Dauntless."

"That is all I ever hear about this thing called Dauntless, nobody seems to care about me. And while you were spending your time with these people, I had to answer the door. Somebody brought a scroll and they would not let anyone else receive it but either you or myself. Very tiresome I was nursing our grandchild when they called, which meant I had to change into acceptable clothing to receive them. All they wanted was a piece of paper signed, why couldn't the butler have done that?"

Before his wife could ask any questions about its contents he saw it as an opportunity to use it to invite her to London. "We have been invited to go to London to meet Government Officials, they want you to attend."

"And when would that be?"

"We should leave this morning."

"Well I cannot go... also I won't go – from what I have heard it is a dirty place full of thieves - anyway I have too many things to do. Also my Bridge Club is tomorrow and I could not possibly be back here in time for that."

Patrick smiled to himself. "I'm sure they will be most disappointed in not being able to meet you."

She was disillusioned in that she thought he should have done more - much more to persuade her. "Well some other time – maybe."

After breakfast he went into his study. Cranking the handle on the phone, he asked the operator to put him through to Max. After exchanging greetings, he asked.

"Would you please organise a Hansom cab to come and collect me, I want to go into the city I shouldn't be there too long. But we are due to go to London, as I explained last evening - I do not want to be delayed by having to look after the carriage and the horses."

"No problem – anything else?"

"Yes order another vehicle for yourself. Victoria does not want to go to London. Go out to the farm and collect Ida. Tell her to pack some very nice things because she is coming with us to meet the London people. I'll wait for you in the club, after which you can take us to the station."

"Oh, that is a surprise I suppose it is her bridge club that is keeping her here. But do you think it is the wise thing to do to take Ida?"

"Yes! I agree with you it is not very wise. But it is what I want to do." He thought to himself, '*Now I am about to lose everything else perhaps I will be able to keep her.*'

While Patrick waited for the vehicle to take him to the city, he took out a sheet of white paper and charging his quill pen with ink he wrote to his solicitors:

Dear Antony

I received the accompanying document which was delivered by hand last evening. As you will see it has a date line to be answered, and as I am going to London today I would appreciate you receiving my instructions for your good selves to reply on my behalf.

I wish to point out that I am not aware of anything in the document that purports to me, and at this stage I am not prepared to answer their insinuations. Please ask for further time so that I can complete my business in the Capital.

On my return I will be pleased to attend a conference with the writer, and his clients, whoever they are, to see if we can dispel the rumours as detailed in his writings, and come to a satisfactory conclusion for both sides.

Your obedient servant Sir,

Patrick Cormack

Shortly after finishing the cab arrived and he left Tullamore, not realising it was for the last time.

When he met his assistant, Max explained, "The first foundation stones for the new housing estate are being laid in the morning. Robert has arranged a small ceremony for the occasion and has invited the work force to be there. He is disappointed that you cannot attend - there has been some discussion concerning who would have the opportunity to move in first - so it has been decided to draw lots at the site and the one who wins will be the lucky one."

"That is very good and a great idea. It seems to be all moving in the right direction." And then thought to himself, *'obviously my son did not want me there otherwise he would have told me last night. But he could understand he did not want his father stealing the limelight.'*

"The real up side is the morale in the factory, it has greatly improved and we are not getting so many faults on the production line." Max added.

**

Wiley had taken the livery on the horse off which was claiming it was carrying the mail. At a suitable point near to the centre he secured the animal to a hitching rail and walked into the centre, to find the agent who hired out staff.

On this part of his journey whilst checking out street names if he had looked to his right he would have seen a very well dressed man, with a top hat entering a solicitor's office. And he would have realised he was the man he so much despised and wanted his revenge on. But his hatred for the girl was deep and he was determined to find her, and looking for the address he had been given was important.

Death for a Starter

The Clerk to the Agency immediately disliked the scruffy individual who pushed open the shop doorway. He strode in pushing two other customers to one side, who had been discussing their requirement with the clerk until he pressed past them and marched over to the desk. Grabbing the agent by the shirt collar, he looked closely into his face. The other was trying to turn his head away from the smell of his attackers' bad breath.

"Now you listen to me, I ain't got time to mess around you tell me very quick where that bitch Roxy...or do you call her Rose lives? And we will get on fine. Otherwise I am going to tear this place apart until I find it. You understand?"

The other well dressed couple left the shop, the lady holding a handkerchief to her nose.

It did not take long for the clerk to capitulate under the storm he was being subjected to and when he gave Wiley the address of the tavern in Huyton the intruder shouted, "I know that you stupid bastard- where did she live before that?"

When the clerk did not have an answer for him, adding, "She moves around and where she works that is where she lives."

Wiley in a fit of rage overturned the desk and pulled a rack off the wall and stormed out. He got as far as the nearest public house when he realised he did not have any money as that had been taken from him. He stormed back and rifled the cash box in the agency before leaving for the second time.

Death for a Starter

It was some time later that he decided to make his way to Tullamore House, buying the petroleum spirit on the way.

Chapter Forty Eight

Ida looked stunning, dressed in a long blue gown with a matching fashionable small hat perched to one side of her head. The two men escorted her to the first class section of the London train, which was waiting to make the journey to the capital, its engine puffing steam and smoke at the head of the carriages. Behind the trio, pushing a trolley with three trunks on it was a porter who loaded the items onto the train.

When they arrived under the large dome structure of Paddington Station, true to his word there was an assistant of Edward Fitch, whom they had met in Liverpool. There was a brief delay while the trunks were loaded onto a Hansom cab, and they were off with the horses' hooves going clip clop on the black cobbles of the London streets, and finally to a luxury hotel overlooking the Thames.

Death for a Starter

Ida was shown to a separate suite of rooms, to change whilst the two men were seated in the lounge of the hotel being served refreshments. Max looked at Patrick, "You must know it is asking for trouble bringing Ida along. What will happen if and when the family find out?"

"Yes you said it before and I know you are right, but I guess I am feeling a bit low. Perhaps one day I will tell you why, but at the moment, as much as I want to - I cannot. By the way please do not mention it again."

Max felt a little embarrassed by the latter part of the remark, he also realised his friend and employer had a problem which he was not privy to. Changing the subject he said, "Is that why you went to the solicitors this morning?"

"As I said I am not in a position to tell you anything. Let us get this meeting over with tomorrow morning, and we will see where we go from there."

A waitress brought over a note on a tray asking "Mr Cormack?"

Patrick took the note which was in an envelope. It was from his solicitor and he quickly read it. "It would appear I have got to get back to Liverpool as soon as possible." He did not disclose the rest of the note which read that the clients of the other party needed to return to New York, but could not go until the matter between them was resolved.

**

After the fracas he had caused in the Agents offices. Wiley thought it would be a good idea to change his appearance, he realised that stealing the Mail Horse was an offence one could be hanged for. After a visit to the public baths, a shave and a change of clothes he looked a different person. The fuel can he was carrying was in a large bag, and after his clean up he made his way to Tullamore recovering the horse he had used earlier to take him there.

At the small cottage, down the lane beside the big house, the two women Mabel and Roxy, had a great day together. One of the stable lads had found a bay for the animal in the stables, the visitor had arrived on. The girls had spent the day keeping busy with the household chores and looking after the baby. As the warm evening's light started to fade, they went up to the main house so as not to disturb Mabel's husband Thomas and also they could see more clearly in the electric light of Tullamore.

They were seated in what was known as the small drawing room, a diminutive comfortable area to one side of the property. Mabel and her friend were happily chatting with Florence, Mabel's mother. The room had two French style doors opening out on to a patio, leading to a grassed area. A tall stone wall on one side divided it from the lane which went down to Mabel's cottage.

With the doors open the three women heard the sound of a horse going down the lane. Mabel remarked, "It is a bit late for someone to be out riding."

Roxy replied, "Funny it was about this time I arrived the other night. Thomas was not too pleased. I suppose he is in bed now, what time does he start in the morning?"

"Yes, so it was. You haven't got any more friends that need putting up - have you?" A tinkle of laughter went round the room. "Tom gets up at three – there is a lot of work to be done before everyone gets ready for the markets."

"Where is Mrs Cormack?"

Florence replied, "Victoria retired to her rooms about an hour ago. She rarely comes down in the evening. She likes sewing and making garments"

"I only met her when I worked here that evening but I thought she was a very nice lady."

Outside Wiley had made it to the stables, and was shocked to find his horse in one of the bays. '*So this is where the bitch went.*' He looked around him and saw a lad standing at the end of the row - looking at him.

"Hi son - where is the lady who arrived on this horse?"

The stable lad had no idea who this stranger was. He had been asleep in the loft when he had heard him arrive. Thinking it was very late for someone to be in the stables, but he looked respectable and did not want to upset a guest of his masters. Anyway he thought, didn't someone else arrive about this time a few nights before. "I cannot say, Sir - but my guess is they are in the main house. But the girl who arrived, she was visiting Miss Mabel who lives in the first cottage."

Thanking the lad Wiley turned, *'The carriage is here, and so Patrick must be. But the girl it seems she is also here. I'll go to the house first and then down to the cottage.'*

He made his way round the outside of the stable block, keeping to the trees and bushes to the left side of a lawn which lead up to the rear of Tullamore. To his right down the far side of the property he could see an open door light spilling out onto the grass. At first he was going to go there but changed his mind and tried another door, which opened into a dark room and appeared to him to be some form of store.

There was another door on the far end of the room. He opened it and he was in a hallway. There was the smell of cooking, so he thought he must be near the kitchen. Deciding he had gone far enough, he opened the can and started to pour the liquid across the floor. His eyes started to water with the fumes. Retreating into the store he closed the door to the hall. He made his way out into the night air still pouring from the can as he went.

He remembered what he had been told and stood back from the petroleum spirit before lighting a match.

In the small drawing room Roxy said "What is that smell, it is so similar to that which the fire eaters use in the circus?"

There was a thunderous roar, the house was shaking. The three women jumped up looking at each other. The noise was followed by an enormous explosion, as the fuel which had formed a vapour in the enclosed hall, ignited.

Wiley was taken by surprise. He had not expected such a reaction. He stood there momentarily and then turned to run across the lawn. Roxy was the first out of the small room and saw him as he was going across the grass.

She turned to the others who had followed her out of the house, "He's changed but I'd know him anywhere - it's Wiley." Wiley turned to see who had shouted.

He was stunned for a moment he had not expected to see Roxy – he ran over the short distance to her grabbing her by the arm and twisting it up her back at the same time dragging a revolver from his belt. "Found you at last, you bitch." He started to pull her across the lawn to the rear gate which led into the lane.

In the cottage Thomas came awake very quickly from the noise of the explosion. There was a small oil lamp burning on a side table which had been lit earlier, so that his wife could see where she was going when she returned. He could equally see quite clearly on the stairway which gave him enough light to recover the shotgun, from its place in a cupboard near to the front door. Cocking the gun he managed to drag a pair of trousers on before opening the entranceway.

What the arsonist had not taken into account was that Tullamore was a small community, farm workers, gardeners, stable lads, waiters and waitresses all of whom had been aroused by the noise of the explosion.

Wiley came into the lane from the small garden gate built into the long wall separating the property from the thoroughfare – he was pushing Roxy in front of him. He stopped not certain what to do as the side road was full of people all going towards the house to see what had happened.

Thomas was also outside in the road his bare chest gleaming in the orange half light from the burning dwelling; he was carrying the gun in the crook of his arm. Wiley's first thought was, '*what is he doing here?*' And then he remembered the whipping and Patrick taking him away.

Holding his hostage close with the gun held in his right hand pointing it at her, he shouted at the crowd, "Keep away from me or she is dead."

The community stepped back giving him space. "I want a horse and trap brought out here – and quick. And no false moves, otherwise she is dead." He was trying to move so his back was to the wall telling the people close to it, to move away.

"Thomas, drop that shotgun." He demanded.

"No Wiley it is going to stay right where it is – and what are you going to do about it?"

Wiley moved the gun away from Roxy and pointed it at his old friend, "Shoot you."

Thomas stood his ground, "Wiley I don't think so - you are in too much trouble now." The look on his face did not give away what he could see behind the aggressor.

One of the stable lads had not moved from his position by the stone wall and was immediately behind Wiley. With a sharp kick which he aimed at the back of Wiley's knee, the leg gave way bending sharply at the joint. The attacker collapsed forward, his gun hand going down to the ground to try to cushion the fall.

He was quickly surrounded and pinned to the ground – a short time later with a struggle some of the men took him into the stables where he was locked in an empty room so he could not escape.

Chapter Forty Nine

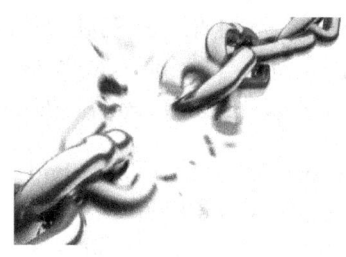

Patrick was feeling very pleased with himself, most of the morning had been taken up with details of the Dauntless motorcycle. However some of the questions he could not answer, and had wished his son had been there, who had better technical knowledge than him.

Nevertheless the meeting went very well, and in the afternoon after a splendid lunch, a contract was signed for one thousand units. The press was invited to the ceremony. After which one of the press people came over to Patrick, "I believe you live in a house called Tullamore?" Max was standing next to him and heard the conversation.

"Yes that is correct - why do you ask?"

"We have had a telex to say that it was burnt down last evening, there was an explosion and the house is destroyed."

Patrick made his excuses to the Government people, telling Max to finalize matters, and added "After which and I do not know how long it is going to take but when it is finished collect Ida – who I am sure is enjoying the shopping - and take her to the Mersey Farm. I'll will go on ahead and I will see her there when she gets back."

He was devastated as he sat on the train deep in thought. His whole world had just collapsed, he had pulled off a fantastic deal with the Army but his personal life was in ruins. His beautiful house was destroyed. Not knowing about Wiley's involvement, he thought it was because some people from New York wanted his estate. He could not fathom out how they knew of the past.

It was not until he arrived in Liverpool and was met by his elder son did he learn of the events. Robert after collecting his father from the railway station explained in the carriage as they made their way to the remains of Tullamore. "It was Wiley who set the house on fire."

"That man has blighted our lives ever since I first heard his name – I should have killed him when I had the chance."

"He used explosive fuel, the same type we use to run the motorcycle engines – it seems he poured it in the hall outside the kitchen, he escaped through the store. There was an explosion which destroyed the main staircase. Mother was in her rooms and could not get out." He wiped a tear from his eye. "Because of the structure of the house being mainly timber the fire spread quickly."

Death for a Starter

He paused looking at his father who said nothing, "Everybody else got out of the house – the maids in their rooms in the attic used the outside staircase. Mabel was with her mother and a friend in the small drawing room, they saw him and chased him across the lawn, it seems he was heading for Mabel's cottage. Thomas says it was the explosion that woke him. He went outside to see what was going on. They managed to restrain him – he is in the jail in Huyton"

**

With a heavy heart and a feeling of defeat, he arrived at his solicitor's office the next morning. After a discussion with his legal team he was told the American people wanted nothing less than the return of the property, which had been sold to his mother, all those years previously. As they made their way to the meeting he was deep in thought, how was he going to turn this to his advantage?

Finally they were sitting around a table and he was surprised to see how young his opponents were. There was total silence in the sumptuous office, waiting for the two solicitors, who knew each other from dealing with various cases, and were discussing matters outside the room. After a little while they joined the others.

The opposing lawyer was a tall well dressed man, with a clipped moustache totally black against his hair which was going white. Patrick recognized him from the Atlas club, he thought to himself, 'I guess my membership is now in doubt –as he knows my history."

The other side's lawyer, without acknowledging that he knew Patrick gave a little cough before speaking. "We have a document which was written over thirty years ago - by a private detective who was employed by the Evens family, to look into the sale of the property known as Evens Farm - to yourself. We are here to see if the sale was legitimate."

Patrick held his hand up, "I never bought the property as you put it. It was left to me in a will."

"Ah yes. But you are now the owner. Am I right?"

"I just told you it was willed to me - so that must make me the owner." Patrick continued and feeling confident said, "Can I see this document?"

The solicitor conferred with his clients, who agreed and he removed it from a paper file passing it across the table.

Patrick looked at it and took a little time to read it before passing it to his solicitor. Smiling he looked up, "Is that it?"

The solicitor nodded and looked totally bored, which gave Patrick more confidence.

"Are you trying to tell me that you are questioning my inheritance and want to take it away by using this scruffy looking piece of paper? Anybody could have made up this story - perhaps it is the start of a play by William Shakespeare himself." He was trying to be funny making light of the note trying to rubbish it,

"We do have other evidence which upholds the facts in that letter. For instance there was a Patrick O'Dowd. We understand that used to be your surname."

There was total silence around the table. After the loss of his wife and the travelling and other events of the last few days Patrick was very tired, the confidence slipping away. "Is that all?" he said.

"We do know that the O'Dowd's came from a place near Tullamore in Ireland. Isn't that the name of your house? By the way I am sorry it has been destroyed and your wife died in the fire. But no doubt the new owners will be able to restore it." It was his turn to smile.

Patrick was looking at the two young people and wondering what they would accept as a settlement. He added, "Anything else?"

"Mr O'Dowd...sorry Cormack – I think that was your mother's maiden name when she married your father – Reuben?" he waited for an answer but there wasn't one. "Well, I will tell you, she married in that little church in Tullamore."

"So some woman by the name of Cormack – and there are quite a few of them in Ireland - marries a man named Reuben, and you think that is enough evidence? It is all rubbish and not evidence as I see it."

There was a pause. Patrick was trying to outstare the other man, but he blinked first. The solicitor said, "So your name is Cormack – was that your fathers surname or your mothers?"

"I do not understand where this conversation is leading. I own Cormack Farm lawfully registered at the Land Registry - so how can these people have a claim on it?" He was nodding his head in the direction of Clementine and Josh.

"We have laid out the details to you why they have a claim on what used to be Evens Farm - you do not appear to have an answer for them. What else would you like to know?"

Patrick was feeling desperate, he could see these people were determined, "The best offer I can make is for you to let my legal people have all the details and we will look at it and see what the answer is. I understand the young couple needs to return home to New York, we will deal with the problem at a later stage and give them details of why I am the rightful owner." He could see that little speech did not go down too well.

The opposing solicitor was shaking his head and smiling while he straightened a paper in front of him. "I have spoken to a judge and he is very willing to listen to the case in the next few days - if we cannot come to an agreement here." He could see Patrick was feeling very uncomfortable. "Let me ask you again. You say your name is Cormack – was that your mothers surname or your fathers?"

"As most women take the man's name when they marry- what do you think?"

"When is your birthday?"

"What has that got to do with it?" Patrick suddenly felt uncomfortable and had a feeling what was coming.

"It is a simple question. When is your birthday?"

Patrick was looking at Anthony, his solicitor, but could not see any help coming from there. "Sometime in May... Why."

"Well I will tell you. According to the Land Registry your birthday is the 15th May." He paused for a few seconds before continuing. "On the 15th May in the same year a Patrick was born to the O'Dowd family in Ireland." He could see Patrick was rattled. "There is another coincidence, the Patrick in Ireland had a sister and her name was Florence – don't you have a sister called Florence?"

Patrick stood up, "I would like to have a talk with my solicitor in private, please."

"Yes, of course, you can use the next room." He pointed in the direction he wanted them to take.

"So Anthony, what is your opinion?"

"It will be a serious problem if you go to court. I think you will lose."

"But they are asking me to give up my life's work. Cormack is nothing like it was thirty odd years ago, it was a rundown shambles. Anyway I was a child, what my parents did is nothing to do with me"

"I understand that. I do not know the answer except that this is a serious problem. If they do not modify their demand, I do not see what you can do. But my advice is to avoid going to court at all costs.

They returned to the meeting.

Patrick sat back in the chair he had been sitting in earlier. He looked at the pair and could see the girl was very angry. He did not know where to start as he did not have an answer to what they were demanding – and yet somehow he had to change their mind. He said, "So what is it you want from me?"

Clementine put her hands on the polished oak table and leant forward threateningly, Josh had moved his hand on to her shoulder to try and restrain her. But she continued, "You have tried to deceive us with the gall of your lies." He could see she was infuriated as she continued. "You!" She was pointing her finger at him. "Or someone in your family killed my Grandfather, and then stole our family property – what do I want – everything that you have because it is rightfully mine…" Her solicitor had put his hand on hers saying, "Enough – losing our tempers will get us nowhere."

"But he asked us what we want and I have just told him – he is a liar and a cheat."

Patrick asked, "Can we continue this a little later, say in about an hour? I need to talk to someone and then perhaps I will be able to meet your client's demands."

The meeting broke up to be reconvened in a few hours.

**

It was a few days later when Ida finally got back to Mersey Farm. She had a shock when she got out of the carriage and saw that her belongings were being moved out of the house. She shouted at the removal men who were loading her furniture and other possessions on to a cart. "What are you doing? This is my house you have no right to move my stuff. Who are you – are you thieves?" She turned to Max, "Max, stop them."

Max strode over to them, "The lady asked who you were and what are you doing. Can we have a reply please?"

The man who appeared to be the leader took a paper out of his pocket, "It says here all this stuff has got to be removed." He showed Max the paper, who read it carefully.

Max turned to Ida, "I'm sorry Ida, but the paper is signed by Patrick."

"But it can't be – they must be cheating and signed it themselves?"

"No! I would recognize his handwriting anywhere."

Ida started to cry, "How could he do this to me, he promised me it was mine – oh I hate him." She leant against the carriage sobbing into her arm. "What am I going to do – where will I live? Max please help me."

"There must be an explanation – we will go to his office and see what is going on." But there was no need Patrick was on his way to the Mersey Farm. The history of his life as explained by the American woman made him feel like a cheat, and depressed him. As he turned in from the lane he could see Ida crying by the other vehicle.

She looked at him in surprise - he looked very tired and very down. Her heart went out to him, "I missed you – why did you leave me. And why are these men here – what are they doing?" She was sobbing as she said it.

"I'm sorry my wife died in the fire at the house, and the house is destroyed. There have been many things to do - I also have another problem. There is a question about my legally owning Cormack Farm. Some American people want everything which I own. After many meetings with lawyers I'm afraid I lost the argument. You will have to move from here."

Her eyes were very bright and she looked shocked, "But you said it was mine – and I could stay here for as long as I wished. Why? Why have you sold it?" she said in desperation.

He could see a tear forming in her eyes. He held her hand, "I was in a difficult situation and needed to come to an agreement with these people. And instead of giving them Cormack Farm I came to an arrangement with them and this place - Mersey Farm - is the settlement. There is nothing for you to worry about. After a period of mourning, we will get married and we will build a new Tullamore, and perhaps rename Cormack Farm as O'Dowd's."

Chapter Fifty

In the purpose stone built meeting house in Huyton, where, amongst other uses, the town council met on a regular basis. The building was also used as a Court house when required. Once a quarter that was its use when the travelling judge, from London, visited to hear the more serious cases the magistrates could not deal with.

Wiley had appeared before the local bench of true men who had remanded him to prison, to appear before the Quarterly Assizes, when a Judge would hear his case and pass sentence on him.

After languishing behind prison walls screaming out his innocence for a little over two months, he was brought before the small council meeting hall, where he waited to hear his sentence when it was his turn to go before the court.

Death for a Starter

The judge had arrived a few days before on his travels around the country attending the various courts. He had read the indictment before entering the noisy courtroom, which went very quiet as the door opened from his chambers. He stepped into the stone hall resplendent in red robes with white ermine at the cuffs and collars, on his head a grey wig which looked a bit dusty.

Justice J.D. Althright brought the court to order by banging his wooden gavel on what would normally be the desk of the Council's Chairman, the noise he made brought the people who were present into silence.

The clerk stood up, which prompted the spectators to shout and cheer, he started to read the names of the accused to appear before his Honour that day.

The Judge waved his gavel, "Alright, alright bring the first one in and tell me the rest when we get to them."

Each defendant had the same lawyer to help with his defence. After the prosecuting council had spelt out the accused crimes, the lawyer, amongst shouts and cheers from the public would try and plead a case for the person in the dock.

The Judge was tired from his journeys and was not in the mood to listen to lengthy arguments, and would quickly rule on the case and the accused person would be taken away, to serve the sentence passed down to him.

Death for a Starter

Wiley was brought in with the sound of chains rattling around his arms and legs. He was screaming his innocence.

The Prosecuting Counsel started to read out the crimes he had committed. Justice Althright brought his gavel down hard on the desk, "I've heard and read enough about this evil creature. This is the man who stole a Royal Mail horse – that is enough to send him to the gallows – and then he burns a house down with some unfortunate woman inside. It is a pity we cannot hang him twice. I sentence him to be hanged by the neck until he is dead."

The defendants lawyer stood up, "Sir, my client is entitled to a fair hearing."

"Sit down I have passed sentence. Are there any more cases to be heard?"

The clerk answered "No your Honour."

With Wiley shouting in the background, his defence council tried again, "But Sir, it is my opinion he is insane, and we should have a hearing..."

"Will you tell the accused to shut up." He shouted - once more he was banging the gavel trying to quieten the room. "I will not have all this noise in my court." He pointed the gavel at defence council. "Now Sir – I say it again I have passed sentence - take him down." Banging his gavel once more he got up and left the small meeting room.

Death for a Starter

To one side of the market square, an old oak tree stood, its strong branches fanning out below the canopy of the tree. One of which was badly scarred with rope burns. For many years it had been used for the same purpose as what was to take place that day.

It was the following morning when Wiley had been put on a horse sitting in the saddle, with his arms tied behind his back. He was lead across the square to the tree. Once more it was carnival time brought on by the spectacle of a prisoner going to his death. There were jugglers and fiddlers all joining in the fun and whipping the crowd into a laughing cheering frenzy. A loud cheer went up when the rope was put around Wiley's neck, the other end tied to one of the lower thick branches that had been frequently used before. A priest standing by the head of the animal, said a prayer crossing himself as he did so. After which the horse was lead away at a fast trot.

Authors Note: Public executions and punishments were banned in England during the period of this story

There are a further two novels in this series

The Dauntless Factor' available at

https://tinyurl.com/y7ye8247

The last in the trilogy is **'The Cormack's'**
available at

https://tinyurl.com/yc9p7jhz

www.percychatteybooks.com

percychatteybooks@gmail.com

www.ingramcontent.com/pod-product-compliance
Lightning Source LLC
Chambersburg PA
CBHW062035170626
46813CB00001B/341

* 9 7 8 1 9 1 6 4 6 9 7 2 3 *